the beasties

WILLIAM SLEATOR

the beasties

Dutton Children's Books
New York

Library of Congress Cataloging-in-Publication Data

Sleator, William.
The beasties / William Sleator.—1st ed. p. cm.
Summary: When fifteen-year-old Doug and his younger sister,
Colette, move with their parents to a forested wilderness area, they
encounter some weird creatures whose lives are endangered.
ISBN 0-525-45598-1 (hc)
[1. Brothers and sisters—Fiction. 2. Wilderness areas—Fiction.
3. Human ecology—Fiction. 4. Ecology—Fiction.] I. Title.
PZ7.S6313Be 1997 [Fic]—dc21 97-6147 CIP AC

Published in the United States 1997
by Dutton Children's Books,
a division of Penguin Books USA Inc.
375 Hudson Street, New York, New York 10014
Designed by Ellen M. Lucaire
Printed in U.S.A.   First Edition
1 2 3 4 5 6 7 8 9 10

FOR MY MOTHER

ESTHER KAPLAN SLEATOR

1915–1996

A SPECTACULAR MOTHER,

A BRILLIANT DOCTOR AND SCIENTIST,

AND A BETTER WRITER THAN I AM

*The author would like to thank his brother Tycho B. Sleator
for telling him about naked mole rats.*

the beasties

one

It was crazy Al who told us about the beasties.

Al was strange; I was his only friend, and I wasn't sure why I bothered. I never knew how much I believed what he said—he often made up stories about himself and pretended they were true. I wouldn't have hung out with him if he hadn't lived next door, and I made sure the other guys in our class didn't know I spent time with him.

"You're going to be living right on the edge of the western wilderness area?" he asked me.

"Not on the edge. In the *middle*." I groaned. "Not another house for miles and miles. So who am I going to play ball with, chipmunks?"

"You can play ball with me," said my little sister, Colette, who was ten.

"Playing ball with little girls isn't the same," I told her.

Al wasn't listening to us. "The western wilderness area," he said in a quiet voice, almost to himself. "That's where the beasties live."

Al had a weird imagination, and he got very emotional about it—that's why he didn't have any friends except me. But I wasn't worrying about his feelings now; I was too concerned about what was happening in my own life.

"Beasties?" I said. "What dumb thing are you talking about *now?*"

"Just be careful," he said. "Stay away from old houses, especially the woods *behind* old houses. And don't get anywhere near any logging sites, new ones or old ones. They're active in places like that."

"What are they, some kind of rodent?" I asked, wondering if we would be living in an old house.

"I can't explain. Just be careful. I don't want anything to happen to you."

"Yeah, but where did you ever hear about these . . . whatever they are?"

"From my Uncle Jim. You met him. He told me about the beasties."

I did remember meeting Al's Uncle Jim. He had been a logger once. Then he had some kind of strange accident that left him with one leg and one hand. "Your uncle losing his leg and his hand—that was because of a logging accident, right?" I said.

"That's what everybody thinks—everybody except Uncle Jim," Al said.

Colette shook her blonde bangs out of her eyes and pushed her glasses up on her nose. "What did he tell you about these beastie things?" she asked Al, her eyes wide. "Does he think it might be *them* who took off his leg and hand?"

Colette spent a lot of time alone reading, and she was pretty gullible.

"I just said *be careful*," Al said.

I was getting tired of this conversation. Remembering Uncle Jim's pinned-up pants leg and the way he fumbled with his crutches gave me a sick pang. I didn't want to think about it. "I'll worry about your beasties when I see them," I told him, unnerved by what Colette had just said. "Get lost, Colette.

Come on, Al. Let's see what's on the Discovery Channel."

Al was watching Colette. "I just hope you'll be careful," he mumbled. "Uncle Jim was lucky. They like children better."

two

Dad was a botanist. We were going to one of the last remaining forested areas in the state so he could study some kind of fungus. We had to do it now, in the autumn, because the particular trees the fungus grew around were rapidly being cut down. Mom was planning to paint; she needed some new pieces for a show coming up and felt the forest would be perfect.

I didn't want to go out in the woods and miss the

first half of tenth grade. I wanted to stay with a friend in town—I had done it once before when they were gone for a shorter period of time. After three months away, I'd really be out of it when I came back. But Mom and Dad insisted that I go. They said it would be good for me.

We would be staying too deep into the forest even for a school bus. But that didn't stop Mom and Dad. They got a tenth-grade curriculum from the school and declared that I could easily learn all that stuff on my own, with some help from them. They did *not* make it clear to the school that I would not be going to school somewhere else.

But I would miss the other kids and baseball. How was I going to stay in practice?

Colette was in fifth grade and extremely precocious. She had been reading entire books for years—I didn't read much. She was so far ahead of her class at school that there was no problem about *her* skipping a semester. And she wouldn't miss the other kids. She read so much that she hardly had any friends. "I learn more from books than from people," she often said in her babyish voice, which made me want to gag. It was a good thing we were far apart enough in age so that we'd always been at different schools—that was why none of the kids who mattered connected me with someone like her.

And now she was going to be the only other kid around for three months, and I was supposed to be responsible for her. I groaned every time I thought about it.

Al skipped class to come and see us off. His eyes were very big; he looked like he was trying not to cry. I was glad no other guys were there. "Oh, come on, Al," I whispered to him, embarrassed. "We'll be back before Christmas."

"Just stay away from old houses and the places in back of them," he said in a hoarse voice. "And don't trust them, no matter what they tell you or show you. Especially with Colette."

"Don't trust *who?*" I said irritably.

"I told you, the beasties," he whispered. "I gotta go now."

I knew I shouldn't pay any attention to this imaginary thing Al was warning us about. But I couldn't help feeling annoyed as we drove away, partly because I didn't want to go, but also because of how worried and mournful Al had been. Why did he have to come along and make everything worse?

Dad hadn't told us much about the lodge where we would be staying. The owner of a logging company had lived there for a while and then suddenly deserted the place. It was a stroke of luck for us, Dad said. No one else wanted to live in such an isolated area, and so there was this house we could use. Dad said he knew we would like it there. "Streams, swimming holes before it gets too cold, hiking trails, cliffs to climb. Everything you could ever want in a country place," he had said. But he didn't know why the original owner had left. And he hadn't said exactly what the house was like or how old it was or what might be in back of it. I didn't want to ask him about that now, in the car with Colette. I didn't want her to get the idea I paid any attention to Al's beastie story the way she did.

After several boring hours, we were way out in the country. Dad had been here once before, but eventually he wasn't sure which road to take and thought he might have missed the turnoff. Luckily, we came to a sort of ranger station, and the guy there told him which way to go.

"Did you see? That guy only had one ear," Colette piped up in her most little-girl voice. "There was that bandage thing where it should have been."

"Yes, I noticed," Mom murmured. "Do you think that means there are wild animals around here?"

Colette looked up from her book again. "Maybe he was attacked by a raptor," she said. "That means 'bird of prey,' Doug," she said sweetly and turned back to her book, looking smug.

"I know that!" I snapped at her. I didn't read the

way she did, but I watched a lot of nature shows on TV. I was glad I hadn't seen the place where the ranger's ear was missing; it made me think of the stump at the end of Uncle Jim's arm and his empty pants leg.

Three miles later we turned off the paved road onto a rutted dirt track. Dad had to go very slowly, turning the wheel constantly. The car swayed back and forth and thudded into holes, and all three passengers were clutching at the armrests. Colette was even having trouble concentrating on her book.

"Not going to be easy getting out of here when it starts to get wet, not to mention snowy," Mom muttered.

"And the isolation is going to make beautiful paintings, you'll see," Dad told her. "This is going to be a wonderful adventure for all of us."

It *was* very beautiful. I stared out the window at hills covered with trees and cliffs of exposed rock. For a while the road followed a clear little stream, with rapids and a couple of waterfalls.

We also passed logging sites, mile after mile of bare areas of dirt marked with the tracks of machines and piles of dead trees. We had to pull over several times when big trucks carrying loads of logs came grunting along.

Dad had to keep telling Colette to take her nose

out of her book and look outside. She would sigh and look perfunctorily out the window, then go right back to the book again.

Finally we turned off the road and drove down a rutted track into a clearing, and there was the house. As the engine died and the quiet swelled around us, we all just sat there and looked at it.

An old house, for sure. It was covered with dark, weathered wooden shingles. There was a wide screened porch in front, and above the porch several large windows with wooden shutters. The shingled roof sloped steeply above, and there was only one round window up there, clearly the attic. The impression it gave was of darkness and age; the round window was like a single eye watching you.

"Rather . . . forbidding, don't you think?" Mom finally said.

I agreed with her. But what I said was, "Oh, who's afraid of an old house?"

"And wait'll you see how luxurious it is inside—I mean, for what they called a camp," Dad said cheerfully and hopped out and slammed the door. "Come on. What are you all waiting for?"

It was late afternoon, the clearing was already in shadow, and birds were making mournful sounds. The rest of us got out of the car and slowly followed Dad toward the house.

The porch door didn't lock. Dad pushed it open and then unlocked the big wooden door that went inside, trying several keys before finding the right one. It was already very dark inside; the porch kept a lot of light out. Dad had to turn on the hall light with an old-fashioned wall twist switch before we could really see.

Everything was rustic and rough-hewn. A narrow staircase led up from the front hall. To the left was a dining room with a wooden table and eight chairs and a sideboard. A chandelier made out of antlers hung over the table. To the right was a living room with a stone fireplace big enough for Dad to step into. Several animal heads stared at us with glassy eyes from above the fireplace, and another antlered chandelier dangled from the middle of this ceiling. Around the walls sprawled a couple of big old couches with Native American blankets on them, and wooden easy chairs and side tables and carved wooden floor lamps were scattered around the rest of the room.

Dad went around switching on lights—not all of them worked—talking about what a wonderful old period piece this was, how cozy we would be here.

I wondered why the last people had left so abruptly.

"Everything's so dusty," Mom said. "Obviously

nobody's lived in this place for months and months; you can smell it. It's going to take a lot of time to keep a big place like this clean—time I'd rather be spending painting."

"What's the matter with you? You know my grant includes a housekeeper—she'll be here tomorrow," Dad said, his cheerfulness starting to fade. "Is that all any of you can say about the place?"

"*I* like this house—it's like an American version of a place from an E. Nesbitt book," Colette remarked, clasping her book to herself and grinning; her hair was falling out of a loose ponytail. She looked at me. "She's an English fantasy writer, Doug." She turned back to Dad. "Maybe you're right about this being an adventure." She looked and sounded happy about it. But all she knew about adventures was from fantasy books.

The kitchen had a big black gas stove and an old curved refrigerator that made a loud, grinding hum and a sink with a faucet that said HOT and another one that said COLD, written on enamel. It was big enough to have a table and four chairs. Everything in the kitchen was dusty, too.

Up the creaking stairs was a hallway with four bedrooms off it and a big old bathroom with oversized white enamel fixtures. Mom and Dad took the biggest bedroom, which had a double bed. The other bedrooms had twin beds. I took the room that faced the back; Colette took the one that faced the front. She immediately plopped down on the bed and opened her book.

"Oh no you don't, young lady," Dad said. "You and Doug are going outside to have a look around before it gets too dark, while we start unpacking. Go on now."

Colette sighed and pouted, but she put down the book and came with me out to the front yard.

Already it was hard to see, it took a while for my eyes to adjust, and it kept getting darker fast. There were a lot of different birdcalls and insect noises; the endless trees made a sound like creatures whispering to each other. We seemed to be in a valley; trees sloped upward on all sides of us. But I could also see swaths on the hillside where large areas of trees had been mowed down; the land there was empty and dead. There were no lights in the distance. I felt a million miles away from everywhere.

Colette didn't pay much attention to the view; she was looking around the yard. The clearing in front was quite small, only ten yards across, and on all other sides trees came all the way up to the house. It was too dark to see very far; there was now complete blackness under the trees. But suddenly

Colette started off into the forest—the forest in back of the house.

"Hey, where you going?" I said, hurrying after her.

"There's something out there." She sounded excited.

"How do you know there's anything there? We can't see a thing." Al had said to avoid places in back of old houses. I turned around to see how far we had come from the house. Only thirty yards, but it was amazing how small the windows were already, how obscured by the trees. I wanted to go back, but I didn't want to admit to my little sister that I was scared.

Fifty yards behind the house Colette stopped. She had picked up a stick along the way, and now she started poking around on the ground with it.

"*Now* what are you doing?" I said. I was more uncomfortable than ever, out here in the woods in the dark, thinking of Uncle Jim's missing leg and hand and the ranger's missing ear. "I think it's time for us to go back. They probably want us to help—"

"Look at this!" Colette cried out. She was standing in a very pale patch of light from the distant kitchen window, waving the stick at something.

"Look at what?" I said nervously.

"Look at *this!*" she said again.

In the glimmer of light from the window I could barely see something on the ground. Several objects, in fact: a baseball and bat and a book.

Colette picked up the book; I picked up the ball and bat. The bat had a good heft. They both looked expensive, much better than the ones I had brought. "Who could have left these here?" I wondered. "The last people who stayed in the house?"

"Why would they leave them here, out in the middle of the woods—but right in the light from the kitchen window?" Colette said musingly, as though this were some kind of game. "And the house doesn't look like anybody's stayed in it for months and months; that's what Mom said." She pushed back her hair and adjusted her glasses. "These things look like they were just put here a little while ago. They look new. And a book and a ball and bat?" she went on, thinking aloud. "Things you and I both like. Like gifts."

"Oh, come on, don't be so stupid; this isn't one of your fantasy stories. Who would leave us gifts?" I said. But now I really wanted to get back to the house, and I didn't care if she knew it. "Come on, let's go back so you can see what the book is," I said.

"Okay, okay," she said. "But I'm leaving this here, so we can find this place again." She planted her stick firmly in the ground and pulled the ribbon out of her hair and tied it in a loose knot around the top of the stick. "All right, we can go back now," she said, as though reluctant to leave.

It took a while, groping through the trees and stumbling over underbrush, to find our way back to the front of the house, and I was fighting panic. I left the ball and bat on the front porch; I didn't want them in my room.

The book was a thick hardcover called *The Golden Bough*, which seemed to be a scholarly treatise on mythology. "Well, that shows they're not gifts," I said. "What ten-year-old would read a book like that?"

"Me," Colette said.

"Yeah, brilliant, wonderful Colette," I said. "It's just because you're so out of it that you read all the time and put down TV and sports."

"I learn more from books than—"

"Okay, okay, I've heard it a million times." I sighed. "But who would know a ten-year-old and a fifteen-year-old were coming here? Who would know what we like? Who would *want* to give us gifts?"

She didn't answer, just shook her head happily, her eyes bright.

But I knew what crazy Al would say: beasties.

three

I had a restless night. I didn't have nightmares exactly, but I kept dreaming about strange voices and waking up and not knowing where I was, as the voices faded. And then I would remember, and I would lie there listening for footsteps in the old house. It was a relief when I finally opened my eyes and sunlight was streaming through the window—especially when I noticed the smells of bacon and baking bread coming from the kitchen.

Down in the kitchen a bulky woman stood at the stove with her back to me. She wore a white, frilly apron and her grey hair was in a bun, and every burner on the stove had something good on it—bacon, coffee, hot chocolate, fried tomatoes. It was a very comforting sight.

She didn't seem to have heard me come in; she stood there doing things at the stove without turning around. Until Colette came up behind me and said, "Hi. I'm Colette."

The woman turned around. She wore a black Halloween mask that covered the top half of her face.

"Good morning, Colette. I'm Mrs. Sloan," she said, and her mouth turned up in what was meant to be a smile—the mask hid the expression around her eyes. "And what's your name, young man?" she asked me pleasantly.

I could feel Colette stiffen beside me. Neither of us spoke for a moment. Then Colette said, "Good morning, Mrs. Sloan." She sounded like part of a classroom of little kids saying good morning to the teacher. "His name's Doug. Why are you wearing a mask?"

"Oh, this." Mrs. Sloan touched the mask tentatively, as though she were embarrassed. "I had a little, uh, accident to my nose. I know the mask seems funny, but, well, you know, plastic surgery is so expensive and . . . I look better this way."

She quickly turned and pulled plates out of a cupboard. "I hope you like what I've rustled up. There's country bacon and toasted homemade bread and jam and fried tomatoes—an English thing but I like it— and the eggs are straight from the farm. Sunny-side up or over easy or scrambled, any way you like them."

"Over easy, please, and I like the yolks as runny as possible," Colette said, sitting down. The table wasn't dusty anymore, I noticed, and there were woven blue-and-white checked placemats.

"Scrambled, please," I said. I wasn't in the mood for runny egg yolks. I really wasn't hungry at all anymore, but the food looked and smelled so good, I wanted at least to try it.

It tasted as good as it looked, and in a few minutes Colette and I had finished. Mrs. Sloan asked all the usual questions about where we lived and what grades we were in and what we liked in school, just as if everything were normal. I kept looking at her mask—especially the part where her nose would have been—and then looking away and wondering if she noticed.

I needed somebody to talk to, and even though Colette was only ten, what other choice did I have? There were no sounds of Mom and Dad getting up; I knew they must be tired after the long drive. And I wasn't sure I wanted to talk to them about the beasties anyway. I also wanted to get away from Mrs. Sloan, who made me very uncomfortable. As soon as we finished, I said, "Come on, Colette. Let's see what it's like outside in the morning."

"But I was going to read my new book," Colette complained.

"You go outside and play, dearies," Mrs. Sloan said, her mouth curving upward underneath her mask. "Just stay out of . . . trouble."

What did she mean by *trouble*?

On the way out, we passed the ball and bat on the porch. In the daylight I could see they were even more spanking new and expensive than I had realized. I picked up the bat and swung it a couple of times. Outside we saw that Mrs. Sloan had a very old and battered pickup truck.

"So what does it all mean?" I asked.

"What does what mean?" Colette answered.

"The missing ear on the ranger and the missing nose on Mrs. Sloan!" I said, irritated by how casual she was about it.

"Oh, that," she said. "Coincidence, I guess."

"Yeah, but what about what Al said? About his uncle's missing leg and hand, and the beasties, and how they like children, and not to go out in back of old houses?"

"Oh, yeah. That's right," she said slowly, remembering now.

"It's just that . . . all these coincidences are adding up," I said. "And then these gifts for us, in back of an old house, right in the light where we could see them. It's almost enough to make you believe it—like the beasties want to lure us into the forest."

Colette's eyes flashed. "Maybe there's more books there now!" she said, clapping her hands. "And more sports things for you. Let's go see."

I could hardly stand being more afraid than my ten-year-old sister—she was probably just too young to get the full implications of it all. At least nobody else was around to hear me say, "Yeah, and end up with a missing arm or something? I want to play ball when I go back."

"What can happen in the middle of the day? And you can bring the bat if you're afraid." She was hopping with eager impatience now.

I sighed. "This is real, Colette. It's not a fairy tale."

She was already heading for the back of the

house, skipping along. I felt silly holding the bat as I followed Colette into the forest. But, as I kept telling myself, at least there was nobody else around to see. And I had to bring *something* to protect Colette, didn't I?

It was very dim under the dense trees even on a bright morning. I wasn't sure exactly which way to go, but Colette seemed to know. And then, in a place that looked like every other place, she stopped and clasped her hands together. "Will you look at *that!*" she cried happily.

There was the stick she had planted the night before. But the ribbon was no longer knotted loosely around it, as she had done. It was tied in a very perfect and elaborate bow, like on an expensive Christmas gift.

The back of my neck tickled.

"No more books or anything," Colette said, sounding briefly disappointed. "But somebody's trying to tell us something."

"Yeah. To stay away from here," I muttered, no longer caring if she knew I was scared. I would have gone back immediately, except I didn't think it was safe to leave her here alone. But I still said, "I'm getting out of here. You want to stay by yourself?"

"How can you leave after we get this message? Somebody's telling us something, I know it." She found another stick and began excitedly poking around in the dense underbrush.

"Don't be such a stubborn brat, Colette! What are you doing? I mean, forget those beasties stories for a minute. What kind of crazy person would come out here in the middle of the night and tie a bow like that?"

"Somebody who wants to tell us something," she said, continuing to probe the ground.

"Yeah, somebody who wants us to come back here so they can cut us up into little pieces and—"

Colette grunted and suddenly stopped. "Wait a minute," she almost whispered. She was tracing a pattern with the stick. "It almost feels like . . ." She knelt on the ground. "This sapling, it looks like it's supposed to be growing here, but there's no leaves . . ." She set the stick down and began pulling at a small tree. She shook it one way, then the other. And then she gave it a hard yank.

A perfectly rectangular section of earth lifted and fell back, supported at an angle by the bare sapling. The bottom of the slab of earth was a neat pattern of boards nailed together.

Colette looked at me, beaming, breathing hard,

her eyes as wide as I'd ever seen them. "Can you *believe* it? A trapdoor! Hidden in the forest, with plants growing right out of it and a handle nobody would notice. A secret hideout!"

"A secret hideout for *who?*"

"And whoever's hideout it is, is inviting us in," she went on, enthralled. "That's why they left the gifts and tied the bow."

"Colette, listen to me, you dope!" I ordered her. "I know some things you're too young to understand. Haven't Mom and Dad told you a million times not to trust strangers? There are crazy people around. Kids disappear all the time. We've got to get away from here and—"

"Child killers hang out at schools and malls, not in the middle of the woods, Doug," she said, as though it were blatantly obvious. "If some crazy person wanted to do things to kids, they wouldn't just sit here waiting months and months for *us* to come along. A normal murderer would go out and *look* for victims." She paused, thinking. "I bet this is just some kid's hideout from years ago or else an old fruit cellar or a cyclone cellar like in *The Wizard of Oz.*"

"If that's all it is, then why would somebody try to lure us here with the gifts and the bow, like you just said?"

But she wasn't listening to reason. She jumped

up. "We'll need the flashlight. It's probably still in the glove compartment. Nobody used it last night."

"Don't push me too far, Colette," I said, trying to sound stern and not pleading. "You know we can't ever go down there."

She sighed. "I just want to shine the flashlight inside and see if anything's there. You wait here and I'll go get it."

I didn't want to stay there alone and was about to tell her that I would get the flashlight but then realized I couldn't leave her alone. "We'll both go," I said, hoping that once we got back to the house I could figure out some way to keep her there.

She rolled her eyes. "You *have* the bat, Doug," she said and raced off toward the car.

I waited. I could have gone back, but I was curious about the trapdoor myself, even though I had to admit that I was more scared than Colette was. It really was dark under these trees, even on a sunny day; the few patches of light didn't brighten things up much. I thought I might have heard whispering coming from inside the hole, but it was probably just the sound of all the trees. Still, I didn't want to turn my back on the trapdoor. And then, finally, Colette came running back with the flashlight.

She switched it on and kneeled down on the ground beside the hole. "Wow," she murmured, shining the flashlight around inside. Clutching the bat, I peered down past her head.

The smooth, vertical walls were dirt. At the bottom of the hole, eight feet down, was a wooden platform. That was all we could see from this angle.

"You're taller than me, and your arms are longer," Colette said. "If you lean way, way over and hold the flashlight as far down as you can, maybe we can see if it turns into a tunnel or anything."

Scared as I was, I was more curious now. And just looking didn't mean we were actually going down there. If she wanted to do that, *then* I would really put my foot down.

I lay down on my stomach and stuck my upper body into the hole and stretched out my arm and swung the flashlight around. And I could just see that beyond the wooden platform directly underneath the trapdoor, a narrow dirt tunnel, full of roots, curved away into blackness.

"There's nothing there. This hole is all there is to it," I told Colette, pulling myself back up.

She laughed. "Oh, Doug, don't try to fool me." In the next instant she grabbed the flashlight from my hand, stuck it into the big pocket of her overalls, and with both hands on the edge, began lowering herself backward into the hole.

"You airhead!" I shouted. I was bigger than she was. I grabbed one of her hands to pull her back up.

Unexpectedly, she let go of the ground with the other hand. The sudden weight of her whole body pulled her hand out of my slippery grasp, and she fell down into the hole with a thud.

"You little creep!" I screamed at her, furious and really frightened now. She was too short to pull out. "I can't believe you *did* this, you idiot! How do you expect me to get you out of there?"

She got to her feet and looked up at me with that smug expression I hated so much. She pushed back her glasses. "You have to come down and help me, Doug," she taunted me. "My big brother has to take care of me now."

I wanted to slam her with the bat. "Oh do I, you stupid brat? I'll just go tell Mom and Dad. And then they'll never let you out of their sight again."

"And what will they do to *you* for letting me fall down in here and then leaving me all by myself?" She stuck out her tongue at me. "You have to come down too, Doug. It's the only way to get me out."

I was almost too scared to think. But I knew she was right. I had no choice. I had to follow her down there.

four

I'd get Colette for this. But I didn't have time to think about that now. Angry and frightened, I stuck the bat in my belt and squeezed down through the tight trapdoor. I dangled with my arms as far as I could, then gritted my teeth and let go. I stumbled when I landed. The bat clattered out of my belt, and I quickly picked it up.

Colette had already stepped off the wooden platform and was shining the flashlight down the slightly curving dirt tunnel. Roots crawled and twisted over the walls and floor. The tunnel was very narrow and had a low ceiling. Colette had to crouch, and I had to bend almost double when I followed her off the platform into the tunnel, trying not to trip over the roots. A full-grown adult would have had to crawl. This place was not built for people.

"How do you think we're going to get out of here?" I said furiously.

"I'll give you a leg up, and then you can pull me up with the bat; it's not too deep for that," she said. "If you were smart, you would have thought of pulling me up with the bat before you came down."

I reached out to grab her, but she eluded my grasp and turned and peered down the tunnel with the flashlight. "Look at how the tunnel curves," she said. "You can hardly see more than a few feet ahead of—uh! What was that? Felt like my elbow touched a wire or—"

There was a creaking sound and a sharp thump behind us. We turned and looked back. The wooden platform under the trapdoor had lifted and was now held upright against a dirt wall. It had been covering a pit, and in the daylight from above we could see that the pit was filled with very neatly sharpened wooden stakes. You could see the knife strokes of the sharpening; it had been very carefully done by hand.

We just stood there staring for a long moment at the ugly stakes. My heart was pounding. Finally I said, not hiding the tremor in my voice, "You're . . . going to give me a leg up on those things?"

For the first time Colette sounded half as scared as I was. "Wow," she said, breathing hard. "If one of them came through the trapdoor and somebody followed it, all it would have to do was lift that platform when it got inside, and whoever was following it would fall into the pit . . . right onto those stakes."

She crept back toward the pit and gingerly reached down into it and very gently touched one of the stakes. She pulled her finger back instantly. "Like a knife," she whispered.

I groaned. "*Now* what are we going to do? How could you be so stupid to come down here?"

"Don't . . . don't get crazy," Colette said, still sounding out of breath. "We'll figure out something. We *have* to. I guess . . . I must have bumped into some kind of wire gizmo that opened the platform. We just have to pull it back down again."

It wasn't easy trying to grasp on the upper edge of the platform by hand, leaning over those spikes. And once we did get a grip on it, we couldn't budge it.

"Locked . . . locked open," I said.

"Yeah. I guess . . . I guess we just have to find the tripwire thing and push it back the other way," Colette said. "It's got to be possible or else *they* could never get in this way. The thing's got to be right around here somewhere; I only went a few feet."

She moved, stooping, back along the right-hand wall, studying it carefully with the flashlight and feeling the roots and dirt with her hand. "Do you think I went any farther than this?" she asked me.

"I can't remember."

"Well, I know I didn't go this far." She moved back again, stroking the wall up and down with her hand. "You could help, too," she said.

"Don't tell me what to do!" I snapped. "It's your stupid fault we're in this hole!" But I did begin touching the wall myself. We knew the tripwire had to be at about the level of her elbow.

"Hey, maybe this is it!" Colette said. She was shining the light on something protruding from the wall that looked like a bent coathanger. She gave it a tug.

The platform didn't move. But there was a crash, and then sudden darkness, as the trapdoor above slammed shut.

"Oops! Guess I pulled the wrong one," Colette said.

"Pull it again! Pull it again! Maybe that will open it."

"I'm trying, I'm trying. But . . . it just doesn't work. I guess you can only open it from outside—or else by pushing it up by hand."

"You stupid little . . ." All I could see was Colette's dark shape against the pale circle of flashlight on the dirt wall. I pushed her roughly out of the way with my shoulder and struggled with the small piece of metal myself. I couldn't get it to move either. "We have to find the other one," I said, panting. "To lower the platform."

We couldn't find it. I don't know how long it took us before we gave up. And every minute I was worrying that the flashlight batteries would run out.

"I guess we just have to . . . keep going," Colette finally said in a small voice. "This tunnel has to go *somewhere*. There must be another way out."

"I could *kill* you for this," I snarled at her.

"That wouldn't help you very much," she said.

"Oh, shut up!" I was dripping with sweat. This was like a nightmare. But what choice did we have? We had to go forward.

"We just have to be careful not to accidentally

set off any other things," Colette reminded me.

"*You're* telling *me* that? *I'm* not the one who got us locked up down here."

We went slowly, trying not to brush against the walls or trip over the roots that snaked along the floor. Even bent way over, my head kept bumping the ceiling. We could see the floor ahead of us in the circle of the flashlight, and often Colette would stop and shine it around the tunnel. We were both thinking the same thing: Every step we took, we could set off something that might open another pit right underneath us. I kept wiping sweat out of my eyes.

I tried to ignore the sensation that the tunnel was sloping gently downward. I didn't mention it to Colette because I didn't want it to be confirmed. If the tunnel was going downward, it was unlikely that it was leading to a way out.

For twenty yards the tunnel curved slightly to the right. Then we came to a fork. Both directions seemed to be the same size, a little larger than the tunnel had been at the beginning. I noticed that my head was not bumping the ceiling as much.

"Great!" I said. "Now we have to decide."

"I'm thinking," Colette said. She paused. Then, without warning, she turned off the flashlight.

I yelped. "*Now* what are you—"

"Just wait. Let your eyes change."

Then I understood. If one of the branching tunnels led to someplace where there was light, this was the only way we'd be able to tell. We stood there in the complete darkness for what seemed to be a very long time, straining to see.

I had the feeling something was watching me, a shuddery sensation on my back. I kept trying to tell myself it was my imagination. But it was not easy to ignore in the darkness.

"Well? What do you think?" Colette said.

"Why are you asking *me?*" I said, having trouble concentrating, just wishing I were out of here.

"Can't we please work together, Doug? If we *both* think we see something, then we might go the right way."

"You don't have to order me around! It's your stupid fault we're—"

She sighed. "Doug? Will you please just concentrate?"

And finally I did begin to think I could see a very, very pale patch of curving wall far down the left-hand tunnel. "The left?" I said. "Is that what you think?"

"Yes. Come on." I sensed her starting to move ahead of me.

"You're not turning on the light?"

"It's better not to, if we can see anything at all. That way our eyes will get used to the dark. And we won't be wasting the batteries."

I was scared, but I was also irritated by the way she always had the clever ideas. Was it because she read so much? I tried to tell myself that she wasn't all *that* smart. She was the one who had opened the pit and closed the trapdoor and gotten us into this mess.

But now, at least, I was beginning to be a little hopeful. The ceiling was definitely higher here; I didn't have to bend over as much, and Colette could stand up straight. And as we very slowly proceeded, feeling for roots with our feet so we wouldn't trip, the light really did seem to be increasing. We turned slightly. And then we could actually see an opening on the left, with faint daylight coming from it.

"Maybe this is it! Maybe this is the way out," I said eagerly. We began walking a little faster. We reached the edge of the opening on the left and stopped and peered inside.

We were looking into a rectangular room. The light was coming from a very small, narrow slit in the far edge of the ceiling, a kind of skylight window that must look up into the forest. There was a wooden ladder leading up to the opening, but it had to be for viewing purposes only, since the slit was too small for anything but a rat to get through. My heart sank. This was not a way out.

There were wooden poles in the corners of the room and also beams supporting the hard-packed dirt ceiling. Oddly designed tools hung on the walls amid roots, things like giant hedge clippers, axes, pitch-forks—and shovels: many different sizes of shovels, from trowels on up. Large, empty buckets were piled up all over the place.

But the strangest thing of all was the old bicycle in the center of the room. It was obviously station-ary, mounted on a wooden platform, held in place by wooden struts. It was hard to see in the dim light, but it looked as though wires ran from the bicycle along the floor and through a hole in the right-hand wall.

"A stationary bike. Whatever lives here . . . you think they're into physical fitness?" I said.

I couldn't see the look Colette must have given me, but I could feel it from the tone of her voice. "Not *aerobics*, Doug," she said. "But if we follow that wire, maybe we can see what the bike *is* for. It looks like the wire might go into a room just ahead along the tunnel."

Just past the doorway, the tunnel curved sharply, and we were in complete darkness; Colette had to turn on the flashlight, and again I had the feeling something was watching me. But she was right; there was another room two yards along on the left. With the flashlight, we looked inside. We both gasped.

This was clearly an important room. The floor was paved with some hard, claylike substance and actually looked clean. In the middle of the room, a foot apart from each other, were two pieces of furniture something like beds—padded rectangular tables a little larger than a person. Except that they were too high to be beds. Above them, three very large lightbulbs hung from the ceiling.

"They have *electricity* in here?" Colette said, amazed.

"The bicycle . . ." I said slowly. "The wires leading from it into this room. I heard about something like that once, a show about some war. Maybe . . . they ride the bicycle to generate electric power? Could that be what it's for?"

"I bet you're right," Colette said in awe. "I read about something like that somewhere, too. Whatever lives down here, they're smart. And you're pretty good, too."

Frightened as I was, I couldn't help being pleased.

It was the first bright idea I'd had since we'd fallen down here.

Colette moved the flashlight. Metal cases lined the walls, old-fashioned with glass doors. We could see what was inside the cases. There were dangerous-looking knives of all sizes, from tiny ones like scalpels all the way up to actual saws. There were different sizes of clamps and tweezers, and all kinds and shapes of ugly, scissorlike instruments. One shelf contained a hand-turned drill, with bits of many different sizes. Another held a large assortment of screws. There were long needles and coils of something like heavy thread. And there were piles of delicate, fleecy gloves.

"An operating room," Colette said softly. "That's where they would need strong lights."

I swallowed, feeling sick, thinking of Al's Uncle Jim and the ranger and Mrs. Sloan.

But I didn't want to believe it. "That's crazy," I said. "Why would anybody put an operating room down *here?* And what would they do with a saw and a drill in an operating room?"

"The saw could be for amputations. And the drill could be for—"

Close behind us something wailed, a squeaky, wavering, sirenlike cry of alarm.

We both jumped and screamed and spun around, backing up against the wall. The flashlight beam focused directly on the figure standing in the tunnel, and we both screamed again.

It was something like a person, shorter than Colette, standing stooped over. Its matted, bristly hair might have been white, but it was too dirty to tell for sure. Its skin was very pale and sluglike and smooth, and the eyes were large, but it didn't look childish: Its very distinctive features were sharp and crafty— long nose, high cheekbones, and almost no chin. It wore a kind of burlap sack tied around its waist.

It could almost have been human, except for the teeth. Two large teeth curved down from the upper jaw, and two curved up from the lower jaw, protruding from its mouth. It kept wailing.

Until a hand reached gropingly from behind it and squeezed its mouth shut. The wailing stopped abruptly. The one from behind made a series of soft but high-pitched squeaks and gave the first one a push. It bent over and scurried away down the tunnel.

This second one was bigger than the first one, but aside from that it could have been its identical twin. It had exactly the same white hair, long nose, high cheekbones, and almost no chin. Just a little shorter than me, it wore an old grey flannel shirt, frayed and patched, and a pair of jeans so faded and worn you could not tell what color they had once been. Now they were the same color as the shirt, and for this reason, and because everything was neatly buttoned, and also because of the twisted metal insignia pinned to its chest, its clothing gave the impression of a kind of uniform. It grinned at us around those extra teeth.

A bigger twin—except this one didn't have eyes. There were two indentations where its eyes should have been and old purplish scars there that looked like they might have been made by crude stitches. Had its eyes been removed? Or had something else happened to them?

And then I saw the knife in its hand and flinched. But how could it see us to stab us or to bite us if it had no eyes?

"Rude enough you come crashing and blundering and blubbering around in here in the middle of the day, waking a housekeeper up—and a lucky thing for you you didn't waking more of the family up, I can tell you," it said in a squeaky, whistling, singsong voice. "Who said you could making entry into our private secret territories? I'm demanding you now. Who invited you? Well? What are you saying?"

I could only gape and try to keep from looking at its face, with those old stitches where its eyes should have been, but Colette, even now, was not at a loss for words. "You did. I mean . . . maybe not you, personally. But something . . . somebody invited us," she said, hesitant, her voice trembling. "Somebody left us gifts, right outside the trapdoor. And somebody . . . somebody tied a bow on the stick I left there to mark the place." Her voice rose. I had never heard Colette sound so frightened. "If . . . if this place is private, then why . . . why did somebody lead us right to it?"

"A pretty Yuletide bow! Oh oh oh!" It giggled sarcastically. "Must have been Blasta, showing off what she can do with that precious right hand of hers. It's way too big for her if you asking me, but she didn't having a lot of choice at the time."

"I . . . I just know that *somebody* showed us how to get in here," Colette said, her voice still shaky. "And then we got stuck inside because of the pit and the trapdoor, and we couldn't get out. We . . . we weren't breaking in or anything. Please. All we *really* want is to get *out!*"

"Yes, yes, please just let us out!" I begged it, my eyes on the teeth and the knife. "We'll never bother you again, never, we promise!"

"First I must see you. Never never will I showing you the way out until I feel a good look at you."

"But please, why can't you—" Colette began.

"Do not move!" it ordered us and, before I had a chance to do anything, it was up against me, practically pinning me to the wall. I screamed; I couldn't help it. It smelled like a ripe compost heap, and its hands were on my face, delicately stroking, going quickly, as if with much practice, down from my face to my body, along my arms and torso and legs. And all the time it was talking. "Yes, yes, two lovely eyes . . . nose a bit big and crude. Open up that mouth! Fine healthy set of teeth, yes . . . nice strong arms you have. And the legs! Running . . . you running very much I can feel . . ." I was achingly terrified and miserable, all I wanted was to get away from it, but I was frozen with fear—and anyway, I had to let it "see" me so it would show us the way out.

It went through the same awful maneuver with Colette, while she stood there clenching her hands, her whole body trembling. "Ah, spectacles, a little problem with the eyes," it murmured. It stroked the flashlight, too, holding its hand over it as if to feel its warmth.

When it finally stepped away from her, Colette said, "Uh . . . now could you please show us the way out, like you promised? Please?"

"What promise? You thinking it's that easy?" it said softly, smiling its feral smile. "You thinking you can just pry out where we live and snooping around and then go bye-bye and that's the happy end of it? Oh, I'm so sorry, my strong, healthy young anatomies, but it doesn't working that way. Oh, no."

"Then how does it work, please?" Colette asked, sounding desperate. "We didn't hurt anybody. All we want is to get out of here and leave you alone. Can't you just please let us go?"

"We would just keeping you here, but we know that might be problem. You will have to going upstairs to your abode for the afternoon. Take rest. Because tonight you will returning here, for the conference, to knowing all the family. And that is when we make our bargain."

"The conference?" Colette said, and I could hear the effort she was making to try to sound polite and conversational. "Sounds like, er, interesting. Um, thanks for inviting us."

Now it guffawed, bending over and slapping the earth with its long hands. It took a deep breath and shook its white-haired head back. "You don't know what we can do, you don't know where we can going, you don't know where all the tunnels and tunnels and tunnels leading. Oh!" It briefly put its hand over its mouth, vertically, so its fingers just touched the eye stitches. "But I give too much away." And then it instantly stopped smiling, and its voice softened. "I just tell you two things: Do not saying one word to anyone about what you finding here. And be back at the trapdoor at midnight. If you breaking only *one* of these rules, there will be no bargain—and you will never be safe again."

Colette and I looked at each other. I was sure she was thinking the same thing I was: We could always just *tell* it we'd be back and then stay away. How could it get us again, once we were out of here? Its threat about our never being safe again could easily be a lie.

Or it might not be.

five

"Stop light source if you don't want to waking the others, and follow me. If you can't see, you can hear-ing."

It started off back down the tunnel just before Colette turned off the light, and we got a glimpse of its peculiar gait. It loped along fast, bent over with its hands slapping the floor, and it clearly knew the tunnel well enough, down to every root, that it didn't have to see to find its way.

In the darkness we followed its padding footsteps and gentle breathing. It was not easy to keep up with it without falling. Colette was faster than I was and went ahead of me. Still, it had to keep stopping and waiting for us. "Can't you propel along any rapider? You both have fine sturdy *pairs* of legs, all warm with blood and full of lovely young bone and muscle and sinew and tendon."

"Seems like you're taking us back just the way we came," Colette said as we passed the fork—it was invisible, but we could feel the air as we went by it, and now the tunnel was lower, and we had to bend over more. "Is this the only way out?"

"The only way out?" It cackled. "Do I looking like a tour guide hospitality person? Do you think I going to giving you a map of the territories *now*, before even a bargaining is struck? You will know as little as possible now. And you will learn and discovering more only as much as it is a necessary conclusion."

It must have stopped because I heard a thump, like bodies colliding, and Colette said, "Oops! Sorry, I didn't see you there."

There was a clunk, which must have been the platform falling back into place, covering the pit and the spikes. Now, having been in the darkness for so long, I could see a faint outline of daylight around the trapdoor above, which dimly lit the area under-neath. The creature dragged over a small ladder, which had been hidden somewhere. It pushed Co-lette up onto the first step. "Up you go, my perfect little body, and push it open with your *two* strong, lovely arms."

It paused. "You will telling no one anything. And you will be at this door at midnight, the two of you, no one else. Then the conference." Its voice took on a rapturous tone. "And the bargain! A wonder-ful, marvelous, tremendous, life-giving bargain! And for you as well. So lucky to be the ones chosen! You will not comprehending until you know the confer-ence."

It paused again and then spoke very slowly, hold-ing the knife in front of it. "Do not tell or try to stay-ing away. Otherwise, you will understand this very well, I promise: You will never be safe again."

"Er, could I just ask you one thing before we go?" Colette said from the ladder. I wanted to tell her to shut up and just push her out through the trapdoor as fast as possible.

"Very curious, aren't you the one? I can imagine all the lovely, intricate synapses and all the entwin-ings of such dainty convolutions in your cerebrum. A question?"

"Is it true that you're called the beasties?" Colette asked.

It hissed like a snake and bared its extra teeth at Colette. It grabbed the ladder and shook it violently. Colette clung to the ladder in terror. "Never, never, *never* speaking that word! Never again!" it shrieked. "We are the family. Understanding?"

"Yes. Yes, please," Colette said.

There was a whisper of wind, and it was gone.

"Hurry up! Push it up! Get out of here!" I ordered Colette.

"Okay, okay." She grunted, and the trapdoor fell open, flooding the place with light that was, after all this time, quite literally blinding. But that didn't stop me from groping for the ladder and barreling up it, roughly pushing Colette ahead of me, squeezing out through the small opening. Outside in the forest I dropped the bat—which I'd been carrying the whole time—and collapsed onto the underbrush, panting and groaning.

Colette carefully shut the trapdoor and removed the bow from the stick. "Don't want to give away where they live," she said.

"I'd put it back if I were you," I said, beginning to catch my breath. I lowered my voice. "It'll make it easier for us to show the state troopers where this place is."

She stared at me, her mouth open, completely dumbfounded. "Huh?" was all she could say, for a change.

"Something the matter with your two perfect little ears?" I said, imitating the beastie. "The state troopers, I said. I mean, we have to tell *somebody*. It's not safe to let those creatures run round free setting lethal traps down there."

"You would *tell* on them?" Colette said, still staring at me in complete disbelief. "But . . . it said you couldn't or you would never be safe again."

"What's the matter with *you?* You're looking at me like I'm something that crawled out from under a rock. Like I'm one of *them*."

"Please don't tell anybody, Doug. Please." She stood over me in her overalls, her blonde hair tousled. "You *can't* tell. I won't let you."

"Colette, what's got into you? Why do you care?"

"I bet now you're going to say you're not going to the conference tonight, either," she said.

"The conference? You think I'm crazy? You think I'd go back down there *again?*"

"Didn't you hear what it said, Doug?" she asked me breathlessly. "How could you miss a time like that? What are the other ones going to be like? What *is* this conference? What's this stuff about a wonderful bargain? I mean, sure, I'm scared, too. Real scared. It won't be easy. But how can you *not* be curious?"

"Curious? To go back down inside that pit with those creatures? It's the last thing I'd ever want to do in my life."

She shook her head at me as though she actually felt sorry for me. "But didn't you hear what it said? If you tell, or if you don't go, you'll never be safe again. Especially if you told somebody like the *state troopers!* They would know right away it was you who did it. Please just do what they tell you—if you know what's good for you. You heard what it said." She stared at me for a moment. Then her face lit up in a huge smile. "And it's an *adventure*, Doug, a real-life *adventure!* Can't you see that? It said we were chosen."

"You bought that line? Chosen? Maybe you're smart in school, Colette, but you can't go around believing everything people tell you. We weren't chosen. We just happened to stumble into the place."

"Yeah, but—"

I interrupted her. "Can't you get it through your head that this *isn't* one of your books? You've got to learn that real life doesn't always have happy endings. And it for sure won't have a happy ending if we go back down there."

"But it said we would never be safe again if we

didn't go. And how many people does something *incredible* happen to? We can't just pass up a chance like this!"

"Let's get away from here. It's affecting your little brain," I said and got up. We walked back to the house in silence.

That afternoon we didn't hang out together, but I noticed every once in a while that Colette had her eyes on me, as though checking to be sure I wasn't going to do anything to give the beasties away.

Mom was setting up her studio; Dad was arranging the room where he was going to collect his specimens. Mrs. Sloan bustled efficiently about in her mask. Colette was watching Mrs. Sloan, too, I noticed. I wondered how much *she* knew about the beasties. But somehow I wasn't ready to ask her yet.

We were both out in front when Mrs. Sloan left. "Did you have a nice time in the woods today, children?" she asked us, staring hard at us through the eyeholes of her mask.

We both said that we had.

"Well, I hope you have a wonderful time here in the country. Just don't get into any mischief." She looked back at us from her pickup as she drove away.

It was just beginning to get dark when we ate

supper on the screened porch, which had old-fashioned black metal lamps with designs of insects on them. Mrs. Sloan had made a big roast chicken with homemade stuffing, and mashed potatoes and gravy, and peas and a salad of unusual greens, and an apple pie. She set it up in the kitchen, ready to serve, before she left. The food was all delicious.

"So, you kids do some exploring?" Dad asked us. "Find any swimming holes or hiking trails or anything interesting?"

"Just a lot of forest," Colette said quickly in her childish voice, before I had a chance to open my mouth.

"It's so nice to be out here in the country, where you can both just wander around on your own and we don't have to worry about violence or gangs or anything like that," Mom said.

"Yeah, it's great." I gulped down some stuffing. I desperately wanted to tell Mom and Dad about the beasties, of course. But I didn't. I was afraid to. But I did say, "Funny that Mrs. Sloan wears that mask."

"Really gave me a start when I first saw it," Mom said. "Poor thing, not to be able to afford to get her nose fixed."

"I wonder what happened to her nose?" I said. "It's funny that there are two people around here who—"

"Do we have to talk about this while we're eating?" Colette said. I knew she didn't want Mom and Dad to connect Mrs. Sloan's missing nose with the ranger's missing ear.

We sat around in the living room after supper. Mom and Dad and Colette seemed perfectly content to read. I was bored because there was no TV. I leafed through some comic books and then paced, getting more and more nervous as it got later.

Colette noticed. "Hey, Doug, let's go and see if the moon's out," she said.

Dad looked up in surprise. "Well, Colette, I'm glad to see you're getting interested in the outdoors and not just books all the time," he said.

There was no moon yet; I could hardly see. In the front yard Colette said quietly, "I hope you're not still thinking of chickening out, Doug. You *can't!* We have to be at the trapdoor at midnight for the conference." And even though she was speaking softly, she still sounded very excited.

"You're crazy," I said. I didn't say anything about missing body parts; we were both avoiding the subject now, for some reason. "I wouldn't go back there for a million dollars."

"I wouldn't stay away for a million dollars—and not just because it's an adventure. I'm curious about this wonderful bargain," she said. "They didn't hurt us, did they? That one beastie could have; it had a knife. It could have stabbed us or pushed us onto the spikes. But it didn't. It helped us get out."

"A trick to get us to come back," I said. "I've told you a million times, you can't go around trusting people so much."

"But it told us to be there. Who knows what they'll do if we don't show up? It said if we didn't go we'd never be safe again."

"You believed that? What can they do? We'll just make sure all the doors are locked."

"You think that will stop them?"

"How else are they going to get us?"

"Have you been down in the basement?"

I had to admit that I hadn't. I had spent enough time in dark underground places for one day.

"I went down there. It has a dirt floor, Doug."

"So what?" I said. But I knew what she was suggesting—the beastie had said the tunnels went to many places—and I didn't want to think about it. "Colette, you *can't* go," I ordered her. "I'm not going, period. It's just too dangerous. And I can't let you go alone. You're my little sister. I'm supposed to be responsible for you, you jerk. Can't you see what I'm really worried about is your safety?"

"It's not me you should worry about, Doug. You

should be worried about what will happen to you if *you* don't come. *Please* come, Doug. *I'm* worried about *you!*"

I shook my head in frustration. "You've got it all backward, Colette. How can you be so . . ." I couldn't think of the right word.

"Oh, Doug! How can I convince you to come?"

"You can't," I said, meaning it.

She pouted and sighed unhappily. "Well, that's it, then. We better go inside." She turned and trudged back into the house. I followed quickly, not lingering, locking all the doors. It was very dark out.

It was also dark in my bedroom. There were no streetlights, no lights from other houses, no sounds of cars. I listened to my Walkman, but that didn't distract me from worrying.

How could I go back inside those nightmarish tunnels? I couldn't imagine it. They wanted to do something unthinkable to us, I knew it.

But how could I let Colette go alone? The way she was talking, it sounded like she might really do it.

I rolled over in bed. Of course, I always *could* just let her go and then say I didn't know anything about it. But if something happened to her, *I* would know, always. Could I live with that?

But she had been warned. She had seen everything I had. She was naive and gullible, but she wasn't stupid; she knew how dangerous it was. And I had told her over and over again not to go. If she went, it would be her own fault, not mine.

Could she be right, that they didn't plan to hurt us, if we went on our own? As though it were a kind of test? After all, we *had* been at their mercy down there, and they had let us go. Could she be right that if we *didn't* go on our own, they had some way of sneaking in here and getting us? But that was crazy, like the fantasy books she read. The only safe thing was to stay away.

I looked at the illuminated bedside clock. It was 11:00 already! Time was passing so quickly. She would leave soon. What was I going to do?

If only I could just forget about it and go to sleep. And if she came back without a nose, or an ear . . . ?

I rolled over again and groaned. But it would be different from Mrs. Sloan, I told myself. *We* could afford plastic surgery.

But so what if we could? I still didn't want her to be mutilated.

It was 11:15 now. There was still time to stop her. Suddenly my indecision was gone.

I got up and crept across the corridor to see if

there was some way of locking her into her room. The door was slightly ajar. There was an old-fashioned doorknob with a lock underneath it, but no key.

My eyes had adjusted to the dark. I stepped inside the room, ready to argue, to tie her up if necessary.

The bed was empty. She had snuck out without me hearing her. It was too late for me to stop her.

But it wasn't midnight yet. There was still time for me to run after her and physically drag her back. I was bigger than she was. She would thank me for it in the end.

But how could I find the way? Even in the middle of the day, it was Colette who knew how to get to the trapdoor. I would be lost in the forest in the middle of the night, alone.

What if I told Mom and Dad? What if all three of us went out with lights, calling her name, making as much noise as possible? That would stop the beasties. They didn't want anybody to know about them. They would have to let Colette come back.

But if I told Mom and Dad now, first they would think I was crazy. Then they would be furious that I hadn't told them the whole thing in the first place. If I had warned them right away, they would have seen to it that Colette *couldn't* go; they would have kept their eyes on her every minute; they would have called the state troopers or something. If I told them now, they would know forever that I could have saved Colette and didn't. They would never forgive me. It was too late to tell them. It was too late to do anything.

I could feel my heart pounding. This was it, then. The decision had somehow happened. I had let her go. There was nothing I could do to stop her now.

Except wait to see when, or if—or *how*—she came back.

I got into bed, more guilty and miserable than I had ever been in my life. Before Colette had left, time had gone so quickly. Now it crawled. I lay there, sick with dread and apprehension, as time dragged on and on.

What was that noise?

The beastie had said if we didn't come tonight, we would never be safe again. It said the tunnels went on and on. The basement of this house had a dirt floor.

Was that a whisper, a chuckle? I huddled under the sheet, reminding myself the house always made noises and trying to convince myself that what Colette did on her own wasn't my fault. The night was cool, but my sheet was soaked with sweat.

I couldn't stand this anymore. But there was no TV to distract me. Maybe I could find something to read.

Next to Colette's empty bed was the book that had been left by the trapdoor, *The Golden Bough*. I brought it back to my room and sat in bed and tried to concentrate on it. It seemed to be a study of ancient beliefs about strange gods and woodland spirits. It was very boring and I couldn't concentrate. I kept worrying about Colette and hating myself for letting her go into the tunnels by herself.

I thought miserably about all the times I had bullied her and called her names and pushed her around. And I promised myself, over and over again, that if she came back and was unharmed, I would never let her do anything risky again. No matter how much she cajoled or pleaded with me. I would take care of her like no brother had ever taken care of a little sister before. I would not even let myself be embarrassed by how different she was from other kids.

And despite how worried I was and how slow time was going, the book was so boring that it actually put me to sleep.

I opened my eyes. The sun was shining; the bedside light was on; the book was lying open-faced on the floor beside the bed. My first feeling was how grateful I was that I had been able to sleep and that this terrible night was over at last.

In the next second a sick pang shot through me. What if Colette still wasn't in her room? What if she was—and part of her body had been taken from her?

I got up and pulled on my pants and paced, twisting my hands. I had to go and look; I couldn't put it off; I had to do it *this minute.* But what would I do if she wasn't there or if she was mutilated? In either case, nothing would ever be the same again.

And still I paced a few minutes longer. Finally I gritted my teeth and took ten deep breaths.

The hardest thing I'd ever done was to walk across the hallway and look into her room.

six

"I didn't hear you knock," Colette said, rolling over in bed and looking up at me without expression.

She was a mess. Her face was smudged with something like reddish dirt; her hair was matted and greasy; she looked exhausted. Still, I wanted to rush over and hug her, except we didn't do that in our family. But I had never felt such joy—and such love for her—before. "You're back! I can't believe it! Are you okay?"

"Where's my book? Where's *The Golden Bough*?" she asked me.

"Colette! Is that all you can say? After you went back into the tunnels? Are you okay? They didn't hurt you or anything?"

"Hurt me?" She shrugged, as though it were a stupid question. "Did you see that book?"

Now the joy and love were fading, and I was getting irritated. I sighed. "The book is in my room. But Colette, why are you acting so strange, so distant all of a sudden? I've been lying awake all night worrying about you. And now that you came back and you're not hurt, it's the best thing that ever happened. And all you can do is ask me about some dumb book? Come on, what happened? I mean, you *must* know how curious I am!"

"If you were so curious, then why didn't you come?" she said. She was looking directly at me now, her hair falling into her eyes, her face blank. "But you didn't come. That was what you decided. I had to go into the tunnels alone. And so that's why I can't tell you what happened."

"You won't tell me *anything*?"

Her voice lowered, as though she didn't want anyone else to hear, even though we were the only ones there. "The conference was very secret, almost . . . *sacred.*" She let the silence hang there for a moment, then became practical again, pushing her hair out of her eyes and reaching for her glasses. "Now can you please leave so I can get dressed and get my book."

I was stunned. She had often taunted me and put me down. But she had never treated me so coldly before. "That's . . . all you're going to tell me?" I said, hardly believing it.

Her face softened, but just a little. "Look, Doug. I think I can forgive you for letting me go all by myself if you'll just leave me alone. But you have to understand. *Because* you didn't come, you left yourself out of something. And I just can't talk about it to anybody. Period."

She scratched her head, thinking, staring at nothing. "You better just forget everything that happened yesterday. You know, the tunnels, Fingers—she's the one we met—everything." She looked away. "I mean, if it isn't too late," she added.

"Too late?" I didn't like the sound of that. "What do you mean, too late?"

She didn't answer directly. "I don't know all the answers. I hope it isn't too late. But it might be. The best thing you could do is get away from here as soon as possible, back to the city."

"Back to the city?" I said, feeling cold. "How could I do that? Where would I get the money? Where would I get a car? Mom and Dad would go nuts. What do you think is going to happen to me here? Isn't there anything I can do to . . . make up for what I did?"

She thought for a minute. "Well, I guess there *is* one thing you shouldn't forget. Something she already told you. It might help you."

Help me? Colette was back, but I seemed to be in more trouble than ever. I was really frightened now. I had also never felt so let down in my life. *This* was Colette's joyous return, after my long, miserable night? She had become a cool stranger. "What? What is this thing I shouldn't forget?"

She looked away from me. "Sorry, Doug. But you didn't come. And you remember what she told you would happen if you didn't come."

I couldn't think. Too many scary and disappointing and unexpected things were going on all at once. "What?" I asked her.

She looked up at me again, her eyes wide but different. "You'll never be safe here."

seven

Colette cleaned up quickly. When she came down, her hair was pulled tightly back, held fast with a rubber band. After breakfast she took her book and went outside. I followed her, carefully. She sat down under a tree, not far from the house. I discreetly kept my eye on her. She seemed to be sleeping more than reading. She must have been up all night.

Doing what? Curiosity about the "conference" was driving me nuts. But this new Colette clearly wasn't going to tell me anything about it. It almost made me wish I had gone.

And so did her remark about how, *because* I had not gone, I would never be safe here. What exactly did that mean? It sounded like some kind of a curse.

I needed to learn more from Colette. She had insisted she couldn't tell me anything, but I didn't think she'd become completely inhuman—not yet, anyway. There *had* to be some way I could pry—or bribe or threaten—a little more information out of her, once the spell of the experience had worn off and she had forgiven me a little more.

Unless they had brainwashed her, or drugged her, or something. She wasn't herself. It was scary.

Worrying, I pretended to study so Mom and Dad wouldn't bug me about it. As the day wore on, I kept thinking more and more about never being safe here and what that meant and how I was ever going to get through the night.

I approached Colette in the late afternoon, when the tree shadows were lengthening. "Hi, Doug," she said, looking up at me a little sadly, as though she felt sorry for me.

"Did . . . you get a good rest?" I asked her.

She nodded and shrugged a little, as though the question were irrelevant and she knew that wasn't what I had come to talk about.

"Colette, can you tell me? Are the beasties good, or what?"

"Don't call them that," she said sharply. "They hate it. They're the family."

She hadn't answered my question, but at least she had told me *something*. That was hopeful. I sat down. "Okay, the family. Are they good guys or bad guys?"

"I told you I can't talk about them. And especially not *here*," she whispered, as though they could hear us through the trees. "I told you, your best chance—if you can't get away from here—is to just forget the whole thing."

"Forget it? But how can I possibly forget—"

"And another thing," she interrupted me. "Don't tell *anybody*. That would be just about the worst thing you could ever do. Just act normal and don't ever—*ever*—give Mom and Dad a hint that I go out at night or where I'm going."

"You mean . . . you're going to keep going?"

She got up without a word and started striding briskly back toward the house. I kept beside her. "What if I went, too?" I whispered. "Maybe they would forgive me for not going the first time. Maybe that would make up for—"

"Can't you understand? It doesn't *work* like that. We went in there yesterday afternoon by accident;

we saw too much; they gave us one chance to make up for it. You didn't take it. So now, what happens to you, it's up to them. You can't change that." She looked up at me, squinting. I realized that she hadn't smiled once since she'd come back from the tunnels. "I'll see if there's anything I can do to help you. I can't say any more than that. And remember—*act normal.*" She turned and went into the house.

I wasn't hungry, even though the leftover chicken was delicious, but I forced myself to eat so Mom wouldn't think anything was wrong. Colette didn't act so distant around Mom and Dad.

"I never knew the forest could be so pretty," she said, putting on her former little-girlish voice. "It's so sad they're cutting it down so fast."

Mom and Dad exchanged a look. "Well, it's nice to see you're noticing things like that and not just hiding inside with a book all the time," Dad said.

"And I really like the way you're wearing your hair so neatly," Mom said. "It always looked so sloppy before, falling into your face."

"It doesn't get in the way now," Colette said.

Her new hairstyle seemed sinister to me.

"Well, I'm all set up now," Dad said, practically rubbing his hands together in excitement. "Tomorrow I start the search for *Aceropala.*"

Colette frowned. "That's your fungus, right?" she

asked him. "You're not going to collect a whole lot of it, are you?"

"Just a few samples," Dad said.

But I wondered what Colette meant by that remark. Mom and Dad were so pleased by her new interest in nature that they didn't think there was anything odd about the changes in her.

And that night I lay in bed and worried more than ever. Was I doing the right thing, not telling anybody, letting Colette go back into the tunnels again? She said they wouldn't hurt her, but that could just be a line they were feeding her—like the line the eyeless one had fed us about being "chosen." Were they brainwashing her? Were they going to take off part of her body? Was I going to have to worry about Colette every night?

But I worried the most about myself, about never being safe here. I kept thinking I heard footsteps and whispers. I kept thinking about the dirt floor in the basement—I still hadn't been down there—and how far the tunnels went. I kept thinking about people with missing limbs.

If only I could sleep! If only none of this had ever happened. If only—

And then my hands and feet were clenched in an immovable grip and at the same instant something slimy and rotten-smelling was shoved far down into my mouth and held there. I gulped, but I couldn't make a sound. The back of the gag was quickly tied around my head, the gag now fixed immovably in my mouth. The hands pinning down my arms and legs were quickly replaced by tight metal cuffs that made a clicking sound as they locked into place, my hands behind my back, my feet crossed. They yanked a tight, smelly bag up over my body and tied it around my neck. Barely able to move—let alone struggle or fight—I was lifted from the bed.

My pulse was going like crazy. Nothing violent like this had ever happened to me. But somehow I was alert enough to be surprised that they did *not* take me down into the basement. The front door was unlocked by a long hand and closed quietly behind us. We headed off into the woods. I still could not see who was carrying me or how many.

Why were they taking me this way, instead of back through the trapdoor in the basement, through which they had obviously entered? The adrenaline rushing through my brain gave me the answer: They didn't want me to know exactly where the trapdoor in our basement *was*. If I knew, then I could block it off and stop them from using it again.

If I ever got back to the house in one piece again, that is.

It was amazing how quickly and quietly they

moved through the forest. Soon they were pushing me through the tight trapdoor, beasties below pulling me down.

The tunnels were not pitch black as they had been during the day. Small beasties hurrying beside us were carrying some kind of dim little lamps that lit up the tunnels and roots, making eerie flickering shadows that twisted as we passed. I could see the backs of the two creatures holding my legs, their short, bristly hair and stooped posture. I lifted my head. I glanced over at one of the beasties who was carrying the top half of my body. It had exactly the same features as the other two I had seen, except for one thing: The nose was much too large, arranged crookedly, not quite in the middle of the face. I looked quickly away.

They took the right-hand fork, the way Colette and I had not gone the other day. Immediately the tunnel began to slope quite steeply downward, and they roughly adjusted my position to compensate. The ceiling seemed to be higher here. We passed dark rooms on both sides of the tunnel, which I could not see inside.

We kept going down and down and down until at last we came to a doorway that had light coming out of it. They hustled me inside and dropped me on a table.

I could see thick, gnarled roots all around the edges of the room. I could see many of the beasties now, standing around the table. And all of them had the same face—the same sharp nose and big eyes and high cheekbones and almost no chin beneath the protruding teeth.

But I couldn't see Colette.

The gag was untied from the back of my head and pulled roughly out of my mouth. I gulped and choked and spat onto the table, and then I managed to gasp, "Where is she?"

"And what kind of a caring are you having for the little one?" the one with stitches instead of eyes asked me. She had not been one of the ones who had come to get me, of course, because she was blind. "You who thought to keep safe for yourself and tolerating her to coming here alone?"

"Where is she?"

The beasties stood and stared at me. I didn't want to look at them. I closed my eyes against the sight of all those identical faces. But I couldn't just lie here with my eyes closed. I opened them, looking frantically for Colette. I kept not seeing her.

What had they done to her? What were they going to do to *me*?

Someone stepped from behind the no-eyed beastie. "Here I am, Doug. Don't you recognize me?"

And then I did, and screamed.

eight

It took me a second to realize why Colette looked so different. The way her hair was pulled tightly back made it look short, like theirs. She was wearing the same kind of grey uniform the larger ones wore.

But at least she still seemed to have all her limbs and features.

She watched as they pulled the sack away from my body and removed the manacles from my hands and feet. I sat up on the table slowly and rubbed my ankles, panting, still avoiding looking at them.

Colette was standing next to me. "What's going on?" I whispered to her. "What's happening? What's it *for?*"

"If you want to have any hope at all, just keep quiet. Don't try to run away. Don't go anywhere. They will decide. Pay attention to Fingers, here." She lowered her voice. "She's second in command. She can speak English. And I trust her."

And then the beastie with no eyes—the one she called Fingers—touched me lightly on the leg, as if to find out exactly where I was. I cringed away and grunted in fear—I couldn't help it. "Down from there," she ordered me. She reached down and found a stool with her hand. "Sitting on stool."

I scrambled awkwardly off the table and sat down on the stool Fingers had indicated. The others at the table sat down, too. I kept my eyes in my lap, not wanting to look at them.

No one spoke. It was like they were waiting for something. And I knew I couldn't just sit there staring at my lap. I lifted my head and looked around at them.

I gulped, feeling sick. There were a few smoky lamps on the walls of this room. The beasties were more disgusting than I had been able to see in my

previous short glimpses of Fingers and the o
who had carried me here. Their skin was so
and absolutely colorless that looking at them made
you think of worms and corpses at the same time.
And the skin was also so thin that you could just
barely see through it. On the smaller ones, who wore
only cloths around their waists, I could see the vague
shapes of bones and organs underneath the skin,
hearts pulsing. Their eyes were larger than human
eyes, without lashes, and bulged out and swiveled,
like the eyes on some reptiles.

And would I ever get used to the fact that they
were all identical twins?

Every one of them had the same features, the
taller ones in uniform, who were a little shorter than
me, and the small ones in loincloths, a little shorter
than Colette. Aside from the difference in height and
clothing, it would have been impossible to distin-
guish between them, except that some were older
than others—and so many of the young ones were
maimed.

There were some with no noses, or only one ear,
or missing hands. Crutches were propped against the
table. Were they for beasties with only one leg?
There were several who had limbs and features—
from whom?—that had been crudely attached. The

one with the nose that was too big and in slightly the wrong place. A small one with a very large, masculine hand at the end of a slender arm. Was this Blasta, who had tied the bow? On many of them you could see stitches and ugly scar tissue where the parts had been attached.

How could Colette stand looking at them, let alone *choosing* to spend time with them? It was incomprehensible. It was all I could do not to throw up. Even if by some miracle they changed their minds and decided to include me—instead of mutilating or killing me—how could I stand to be included in anything having to do with *them?* They were just too gross.

Every one of them had a clay mug, from which it took frequent sips. Colette was drinking from a mug too. What was the stuff? Was it something that had brainwashed her? I was glad they weren't trying to make me drink it.

There was the sound of slow, dragging footsteps from out in the corridor. All the beasties rose instantly to their feet, some grabbing their crutches for support.

"Stand up!" Fingers hissed at me. "The Queen! She comes up here tonight, even after tragedy today." Fingers prodded me. I jumped to my feet, wondering why she said "up here" when we were so deep inside the earth.

A great creature, taller than a human adult, tottered into the room, supported by an elderly small beastie on either side of her. She had the same face they all had, though hers was heavily made-up. Lipstick smears stained her protruding teeth, like blood; she wore rouge and eye shadow and dangly earrings of some dull metal. She was the only one you could immediately tell was female.

But the big difference between her and the rest of them was her size. She was at least three heads taller than any of the others and a lot bulkier. She wore a long robe, but by the contours underneath it you could tell that there was a great deal of loose flesh on her body. It was as though her skin was a series of deflated inner tubes hanging there.

She sank into a chair at the head of the table. She said something stern in a voice that was deeper than the others' and slightly hoarse. Everyone sat down, so I did, too.

The Queen looked sick, despite all the makeup she was wearing. I could see that she wasn't maimed, but there still seemed to be something wrong about her body. I wanted to ask Fingers but I didn't dare; everybody was sitting in hushed silence.

The Queen drank deeply from her cup, which was larger than the others. She pulled a clipboard toward her with one hand; her fingernails were bright red. She uttered a resonant syllable. A beastie squeaked the same syllable. The Queen uttered a different word; a different beastie repeated it. This went on for a while before I realized what it was: roll call.

I noticed that there were charts all over the walls, though they were incomprehensible to me, and also maps. For creatures so monstrous-looking, they seemed to be very well organized.

Why had they brought me here?

As soon as roll call was over, the Queen looked directly at me. She spoke what was clearly a command.

"Up on table but standing now, so all to seeing your muscles and joints and digits and features," Fingers told me.

I realized I had on nothing but my underwear. I was shy. I didn't move.

"Hurry! Do what Queen says," Fingers whispered and poked me hard with her fist.

I climbed back up on the table and stood there, blushing, feeling horribly exposed in just my boxers. They all looked at me fixedly with their large, fishy eyes, not embarrassed to stare. And then, even worse, the younger ones—the ones missing things—began whispering, pointing at me with stumps.

The Queen issued another command. "Enough!" Fingers said. "Again sitting." And I got back down to my stool with immense relief.

And then the Queen seemed to forget about me. She turned to the beastie sitting next to her—a young one, especially tall and strong-looking—and she smiled. It was a horrible sight, with her sagging features and heavy makeup and those red-stained, rodentlike teeth. She smiled and rubbed her big, loose body against the other beastie's shoulder. The other beastie's skin flushed slightly, a purplish color. It opened its mouth wide and emitted a sharp hiss.

It seemed to be the right response. The Queen smiled more broadly and nodded approvingly.

And then, suddenly, she was all business again. She turned back to Fingers and issued a long stream of angry words, her earrings shaking.

"She say we smashing one of our very most important rules, to allowing you here, when you willingly did not come. This we do because of our recent tragedy and our lively esteem of Colette, who is your sister—though the resemblance we are not seeing in your look or your action."

So Colette was wonderful, and I was ordinary, as

usual. Scared as I was, I was also beginning to feel resentful.

"So we are not . . ." Fingers paused. "Uh, are not *yet* doing the thing we in the normal doing to those who discover us and who do not first of all willingly side with us. Because of tragedy and esteem of Colette, we are not yet doing. She promise we can endowing you our trust." She waited. "Well? What your cerebrum thinking of what she say to us?"

What choice did I have? "Sure, sure, you can trust me," I said quickly.

Fingers and the Queen exchanged more words.

Fingers said to me, "Queen say human children are of use to us in reconnaissance missions—of more use far than human adults, who cannot be trust. We hoping we made risk to broken our rule for good reason, and you will be of very abundant helping to Colette in mission tomorrow."

"Mission?" I turned and looked at Colette, who was sitting across the table from me, her chin just above the surface. What had she gotten me into? I was on the verge of protesting. Then I remembered what the Queen had said about something they usually do to people who discover them and don't side with them. Maybe this mission, whatever it would be, was the lesser of two evils.

They were all watching me as they sipped from their cups, waiting for me to agree or disagree with this order the Queen had given me. I turned back to Fingers. "Excuse me," I said hesitantly. "But you're talking about missions and reconnaissance. Words like that make it sound like you're . . . you're fighting some kind of war."

Fingers lifted her head and spoke to the group, as if translating what I had just said. There was a moment of stunned silence. Then they were all laughing and hooting and slapping the table, as though I had said the most ridiculously obvious thing in the world.

As the laughter died away, the Queen gave Fingers another sharp, angry command. Then she turned away and smiled flirtatiously and sidled up to the young beastie beside her again.

"Come, human children, Queen want us to going now," Fingers said. In an instant she and Colette were up from their seats and on their way out of the room. I sat there stupidly for a moment until it hit me that I was supposed to be going with them—the Queen wanted us out of there. By the time I got out into the tunnel, they were ahead of me.

The tunnel continued to slope steeply downward, and I couldn't see. There were no lights here, and of course Fingers didn't need one, and Colette seemed to be trotting along right beside her. I could hear them whispering together as I stumbled along behind their voices. Were they talking about me? Making fun of me?

Colette appeared to know the tunnels as well as Fingers did. So why was she with her and not guiding me? I was confused by what had gone on at the conference; I felt left out and even *jealous* of how friendly Colette and Fingers seemed together. I wondered again what had happened last night that already Colette seemed to be so much a part of the beasties. As gross as the beasties were, I felt even more resentful now about being the ordinary one, the begrudged one, while Colette was the one who impressed them and who was eagerly included.

I tripped over a root and fell flat on my face. It hurt, and I couldn't help groaning as I struggled to my feet.

"Will we waiting for the slow one *forever?*" Fingers complained.

"Come on, Doug, hurry it up," Colette said.

"How do you expect me to see in these tunnels without a light?" I demanded. "And what was wrong with the Queen? She looked sick. What did she mean about a tragedy? And why was she *flirting?*"

"She just lost a litter. The pups were all born dead. Now will you be polite and shut up about it?" Colette whispered angrily, suddenly beside me. "You don't know how lucky you are. And fuel for lights is hard to get; they can't waste it. Come on, I'll guide you. Put your hands on my shoulders." I did as she said. She led me forward.

"But what do you mean about the Queen losing—"

"*Shhhh!*" Colette hissed. "Don't mention it again."

I could hear Fingers snickering in the darkness ahead, laughing at me for sure now. How could Colette be *friends* with that gross, disgusting freak?

After what seemed to be forever, we finally made a sharp left into what must have been a doorway in the blackness.

"Fuel precious, yes, but you two must seeing now, so look quickly what I am showing, and do not waste," Fingers said. We could hear her fumbling around, feeling for things. A small light flickered to life, illuminating Fingers' stitched face from below, making it even more ghastly. I looked quickly around. This room was smaller than the conference room, and four hammocks were strung from wall to wall, a kind of dormitory. Next to the doorway, against a wall, was a small table; the light on the table came from a little clay vial with a wick and an oily smell.

There was a chart on the table, which seemed to be made of some kind of smoothed, flattened bark. Lines were carved into the surface of the chart, lines that Fingers could feel and Colette and I could see.

"This your house." Her finger touched a neat rectangle on the chart, then moved away. "Here trapdoor twelve, the one you used—now you know the scale, the size of this picture. Here road from your house, and down here, logging site. Over here across from it is the dry streambed, where was once water, before the slaughter. You are taking all in, Col? You will knowing to find outside?"

"Easy. Go on."

Fingers wasn't asking *me* if I understood; it was like I wasn't there, and she and Colette were acting like best friends. And why couldn't I mention what had happened to the Queen? They were treating me like dirt. It made me mad.

"You do not going to logging site by road, oh, no, no, because then they maybe think you *want* to going there. They must not know that; they must not know anything. They think you taking a happy little hike in the pretty forest, and pass the dry streambed, and then come by obscure accident to the place where they kill our home. They think you lost, you needing help. Oh, the poor little children! You looking and seeing everything very quick, and you do not let them see you looking, because the enemy very afraid. They do not know what they afraid of. But we do." She nudged Colette, and they both chuckled.

"What's so funny?" I said sourly. I felt sick and left out. And I was remembering that Al had told us to avoid logging sites.

They ignored me. "We do not thinking they are afraid of human children, so that is why you are to going. And you must be like you are stupid, like you do not know *anything*. Very important, very important."

Fingers reached out with her hand, her head tilted upward, groping the air, and suddenly found my chin and grabbed it. "Do you understanding that, Doug *brother*?"

I jerked, startled by her unexpected touch. I was also angered by the sarcastic way she said my name. But, again, what choice did I have? "Okay, okay, we don't know anything."

She let go of my chin. "It will be late in the daylight when you coming upon the place, after the enemy have stopped the slaughter," she continued in her breathy voice. "Your fresh young synapses will exactly remembering the location of all weapon and machine, and you will remembering also exactly which rooms in the sleeping place are the humans—there are not so many humans there now, because of their fear." She laughed again, and again Colette joined her.

"What's so funny about—" I started to ask, but she interrupted me.

"You remembering the location now? You have see enough?"

"Take a good look, Doug," Colette told me. "Something might go wrong and you might have to think for yourself."

She said it as though my having to think for myself was the worst-case scenario. She was getting more insulting by the minute. "Will you stop acting like I'm the stupid one?" I snapped.

She sighed. "Just memorize the map, Doug."

"But I don't understand what the point is. Why do we have to go to this logging site? Why do we have to act ignorant? What's going on, anyway? What did you mean about the Queen losing—"

Fingers made a threatening hissing noise.

"Listen to me, Doug," Colette said, closing her eyes briefly, trying to be patient. "They're letting you off, giving you a chance, because they need help now, and I told them I needed you to help me. Don't forget that, and concentrate. Can you remember this map?"

"Sure I can," I insisted, studying the map, trying to concentrate, which wasn't easy in this situation.

Until suddenly Fingers blew out the light. "Wasting fuel," she said. "If you needing more time than that, then to us you are not of use. Now go to sleeping in your lovely pillows. You will need for mission tomorrow. Leave information at trapdoor twelve, quick as you get back. The others . . ." She hesitated, and her voice changed. "The others will be able to reading it. And then *our* mission begins."

But she didn't say it excitedly. She sounded in pain. And I was struck by an odd insight, for me. Whatever their mission was, Fingers wouldn't be able to go on it. Because she couldn't see. And she minded. She minded a lot.

nine

I could see by my illuminated watch that it was only one A.M. when we exited the trapdoor, from the stale closeness of the tunnels out into the moving air and the vastness of outside.

"Why aren't you staying there all night again?" I asked Colette.

"I need to rest for the mission tomorrow." She started off quickly toward the house.

"But what *is* the mission?" I asked, crunching

and stumbling through the underbrush after her. "Why is it so important for us to go snooping around this logging site?" Al had warned us against the woods behind old houses, and we had gone there, and look what had happened. He had also warned us against logging sites. How much worse was this going to get?

Colette stopped and turned around to face me with her hands on her hips. "You don't have to know everything, Doug. *I* don't know everything." I wondered how true that was. "You just have to know that this is the way I saved you, by getting them to give you the chance to do this. It's a test. And if you don't pass it, you'll be in the same boat as the other people who discovered them and didn't side with them on their first chance." She started walking again.

I hurried after her. "But what happened to those people? Why do there have to be so many secrets? What did you mean about the Queen's litter?"

She stopped again and stamped her foot. "Oh, why did I tell you *anything*? Stop thinking about what you're not supposed to know. Think about the map. I'm drawing a picture of it when I get back to my room, and you should, too. And then get a lot of sleep."

"Why are you so different now?" I asked her.

"You're acting so tough all of a sudden—ever since you went down there." I didn't want to say what I was really feeling, which was that she was being mean to me, and it hurt. A week ago I wouldn't have noticed or cared—I would have just insulted her back. Now, in this weird situation in the middle of the woods, I felt a little different.

She sighed. "Since when were you so sensitive, Doug? And don't tell me I'm being mean. I'm trying to save you. So you have to be careful with them. Like seen and not heard. And you kept asking dumb questions down there; you've got to learn not to do that. Just do what they tell you. And do it the best you can. And then maybe—*maybe*—things will work out okay for you."

We set out at four the following afternoon.

"Where are you going, dearies?" Mrs. Sloan asked us as we were on our way out the door.

"For a walk," Colette said. I could tell she was itching to get away from her.

"Well, be sure not to get lost," Mrs. Sloan told us. "Don't want to get lost in the woods around here, do we?"

We assured her we would be careful and hurried out.

"Did they tell you anything about her nose?" I whispered to Colette.

"No," she said, obviously not wanting to talk about it.

It was an overcast day, and windy; leaves rustled all around us as we made our way through the dimness of the uncut part of the forest. It would still be light enough to see well by the time we got to the logging camp, but they would have stopped work for the day, Colette said.

"Why is it so important that we get there after they've stopped?" I asked her.

"So we can see where they've left their equipment for the night and see what quarters the men will probably be sleeping in."

"Why do the beasties want to know those things?"

"Don't *call* them that!" she whispered, looking around. Again, it was as though they could hear us through the trees. "And don't ask so many questions. If you can prove that you're useful to them, then maybe you'll be safe. That's all you need to know. And the less you know, the safer you'll be."

We both had the maps we'd drawn last night, our versions of what Fingers had showed us in the underground dormitory. Mine was a lot neater than Colette's because I was five years older. I also felt mine was more accurate in terms of scale and distance. And it wasn't long before we began arguing about which way to go.

"We should start heading over to the right," Colette said. "We've come about twice as far as the distance from the house to the trapdoor, and that's how far my map says it is."

"We haven't come that far," I told her, looking at my map. "And you're forgetting about the dry streambed."

"I am not forgetting about the dry streambed," she said, very slowly and clearly, as though talking to an idiot. "But it looked like it went all over the place. Accurate distance is more important."

"Fingers said we turn right toward the logging camp *after* we pass the dry streambed," I reminded her. "And according to my map, it's farther than this."

"According to my map, we should turn here," she said. "Fingers trusts me more than you."

"Well maybe I don't care what your wonderful buddy Fingers thinks," I snapped at her. "What does she know about accurate distance? She's blind."

Colette rolled her eyes. "She could feel it on the map. And she was born here, Doug. Even if she can't see now, she knows more about the layout than *you* do."

"Well, I don't trust her one bit. We're not supposed to go near logging sites, Al said. I bet Fingers is setting us up, leading us into some kind of trap. How can you trust somebody who looks so gross?"

"What difference does it make what she looks like? How can you trust somebody like Al, who's always making things up just to get attention from dummies like you who believe him?"

"I didn't say I believed him about *everything!*" I shouted at her. "And he didn't make up his Uncle Jim's missing leg and hand. What about *that?* What does Fingers have to say about *that?*"

She reached up and put her hand over my mouth. "For once, could you please not be such a *dope,* Doug?" she whispered, breathing hard. "You don't know where the tunnels go; you don't know what they can hear. The only reason you're on this mission and not . . . uh, somewhere else is because I lied to them that I needed you to help me. To save you." She looked away from me and scowled. "I probably shouldn't even have let you come; I should have let you stay at home and do whatever you do when you're not watching the Discovery Channel. But I thought it would be more honest to the family if I brought you along, since I told them I needed you." She looked up at me again; the way her hair was pulled tightly back made her face look hard and older. "I didn't expect you to be an asset, but could you at least *please* not be a liability?"

She was such a different person now than she had been at home! She even talked differently. What had the beasties done to make her like this? Again, I wondered about brainwashing. Was it that drink?

"I'm *trying* to be an asset," I told her. "And I know about following maps and directions. Solid landmarks are more important than guessing about distances."

"Fine. Have it your own way," she said. She started walking again.

She was admitting that I was right, even though she refused to say it in so many words. But that didn't mean I still wasn't angry. Angry that she acted so superior, angry that she and that freak Fingers were so buddy-buddy, and especially angry that she obviously knew a lot that she wasn't telling me.

Like the purpose of this mission, for instance. If they wouldn't tell me what the purpose was, then why did I have to follow all their orders, like not to give anything away? I could sabotage this mission if I wanted to. *That* would show Colette and Fingers and the rest of them how superior they were.

Colette turned and looked at me, studying my face. "And don't you dare try to screw this up, Doug," she said, just as if she could read my mind. Were my mental processes that predictable? Or had she gotten smarter somehow? "Because if you do anything wrong," she said slowly, "the consequences will be worse than you can imagine—for both of us. I think the best idea is for you to just keep your mouth shut and let me do the talking."

I was seething inside. I turned angrily away from her. And then I pointed. "See? The dry streambed," I said. "Just like it says on my map."

Again, she refused to admit that I was right. She just grunted.

We reached the streambed, a dusty gully full of dirty rocks. Colette stopped and stared at it thoughtfully. "Think of what this was like when there was water in it and fish and frogs and everything, before they started cutting down the trees," she said. "It makes me angry and sad at the same time."

Last night at dinner she had also talked about how sad it was that the trees were being cut down. She had never expressed any interest in nature or the environment before the beasties had gotten their hands on her.

We crossed the streambed and turned right. Soon we could hear the labored rumble of machinery. And then we saw up close what was going on here.

There was a very sharp line where the day's work had ended. It was like stepping out of the forest right into a kind of desert. Clearly, they weren't cutting down the trees one at a time, leaving the smaller ones to grow; they were just plowing down everything there was, as fast as possible. We were under the trees and picking our way through underbrush one minute, and the next there was nothing around but dirt, full of stumps. And even though the day was overcast, it was a lot brighter here.

Machinery was still moving, hauling felled trees, directly in front of where we were standing.

Colette grabbed my elbow and pulled me back under the trees. "We don't show up until they've stopped working, remember?" she said.

I hadn't remembered because I was interested in seeing how the machinery worked. And I was angered even more by the way Colette just pulled me back under the trees, as though she were the boss. That was what she believed, anyway. She had made it clear that it was only because of her intervention that I was here and not someplace worse, and for that reason I had to do what she told me to do.

But we hadn't reached the logging camp yet.

"We came out of the woods just exactly where we

were supposed to, where the trucks and tractors are," I pointed out. "If we'd turned where you wanted to, we'd be much farther from the camp now."

"You always have to be right about something, don't you?" she said. But she didn't deny that I *was* right. I was just better at maps than she was, period.

In the shadow of the trees, we both looked at our watches. "It's after five; they should be stopping soon," Colette said.

Again, I wanted to know why it mattered to the beasties to know where the loggers left their equipment for the night, but now I was too proud and angry to ask. I just stood there and waited, holding the anger in, letting it grow.

After about fifteen minutes, the noises stopped. We could see men climbing out of the cabs of their vehicles. There was still plenty of light, but the men did not linger; they did not stroll. They walked purposefully away from the forest.

Colette pulled the rubber band out of her hair and shook it loose, making herself look childish like before. "Let's go," she said, and we started out of the woods and across the dirt. "We're lost, remember?" she said, and I nodded. I didn't like following her orders. But she wouldn't be able to boss me around in front of other people.

We reached the closest piece of equipment. Colette looked around to be sure no one was watching, then squatted down behind it and took a notebook out of her overall pocket. She made a quick note, put the notebook away, and we started off again.

There were stumps all over the place and piles of dead trees. And ahead there were low wooden buildings, surrounded by a very high cyclone fence. As we got closer, we could see that the fence had swirls of shiny barbed wire along the top. There was a gate in the fence and beside it a small building like a guardhouse. The last men going through the gate paused routinely to show something to whoever was inside.

"We better hurry," Colette said. "After they've all gone through, they might close the guardhouse and we won't be able to get in." She began to jog, and I jogged with her.

The gate was locked when we reached the guardhouse. The top half of the door was open, and we could see that there was a tall, heavyset man inside, doing some kind of paperwork with big, strong hands.

Colette gave me a firm look, her finger over her mouth. She rubbed her eyes with her fists until they were red. And she said—in her sweetest and most pathetic little voice—"Sir? Excuse me, sir?"

The man jerked in his seat and dropped some papers off the table. He seemed more than just startled; he seemed frightened, too. He was holding a rifle when he looked out the window. "Who's there?" he said sternly. Even when he saw Colette, his expression didn't soften.

"Please, sir," Colette said, sniffling. "We just went for a little walk. And now we're lost. And it's getting dark. And we don't know how to get home. And we're afraid."

"I'm not afraid," I said.

The man looked at me for the first time. His expression didn't change; his face was still hard and suspicious.

"Must have been a mighty long walk you two kids were on," the man said. "No families living around here, far as I know."

"We just moved here the other day," Colette explained, wiping her eyes. "That's why we don't know our way around. We live in the old house with the big porch in front and the round window in the attic. The owner of a logging company used to live there, I think. Our father's doing research on . . . what is it, Doug?"

She knew very well what his research was, but she was acting dumb. "Fungus," I said. "That's why we came here in the fall."

"I'm so afraid," Colette said again, and her voice broke.

The man put down the rifle and nodded slowly, holding his stubbled chin. His expression began to soften. "So there's a family staying in the old Beardsley place. You say your father's a scientist?"

"A botanist," I said. "I think it's cool to be living out here, but Colette's afraid." I was playing along with Colette's plan, which I hadn't intended, but it made me feel good to tell someone Colette was afraid and I wasn't.

"Well, sometimes there might be things to be afraid of," the man said guardedly. "Somebody ought to tell your folks not to let you go out in the woods so close to dark."

"Things to be afraid of? Like what?" I said, knowing Colette would hate me for this and glad of it— my anger wasn't *completely* gone yet. "Like weird animals that live in the woods, maybe? Or maybe something that isn't—"

Colette pinched me hard in the butt at the same moment she burst into tears. "I just want to go home," she sobbed, her hair falling into her eyes. "As fast as possible, as quick as possible. Please, can you help us?"

"It's okay, honey, don't worry," the man said kindly. "The best way for you to get home is up the road, and that's on the other side of the camp. My orders are not to let anybody in without ID. Not anybody. But then you'd have to walk all the way around the fence out there, much farther than going straight through the camp on the inside." He folded his arms across his chest, thinking. "Well, hell, I can forget the rules just this once, for a couple of lost kids," he said. He pressed his lips together, as if still trying to decide. Then he opened the bottom half of the door and came out carrying a big set of keys—there were several locks on the gate, for extra security.

"Do all logging camps have security like this?" I asked the man as he worked at unlocking the gate.

"Around here they do," the man said, as though he didn't want to talk about it.

"Why?" I pressed him, knowing Colette was hating it. "What happened here?"

"Nothing happened here, and nothing will. It's because of what happened at the other camps. We don't talk about it."

He stopped, the last padlock still unopened. He was deciding whether or not to let us in after all, because of my questions. Colette would be furious—she had told me not to say anything. She whimpered again, even more pathetically.

The man turned the key and pulled open the gate. "Come on," he said gruffly.

We stepped inside. Colette was still pretending to wipe her eyes, but I could see that she was really looking around. There was still plenty of light, but the lights were on in some of the barracks—it must be darker inside them. There were a lot of trucks around and piles of trees and other machinery.

This was the important part of our mission—to remember and tell the beasties where everything in here was. On the way over, fighting with Colette, I had decided I would do everything I could to interfere with the beasties' plans. Now, after seeing all this security and how this tough logging guy had been so afraid at first, I wasn't sure what to do. If I purposely botched the mission, the beasties would get me for it. Colette had said so, and I believed her. And the way they would get me would be gruesome.

But if I *helped*—as Colette had told them I would—if I even remembered a few details that Colette didn't, then maybe their attitude toward me would change. Maybe they would respect me, the way they respected Colette.

Respect me? Why did I care what those freaks thought about me? And whose side was I on, anyway? The loggers were human; the beasties weren't. Who should I be loyal to?

But it wouldn't hurt to look around and try to remember as much as I could. Later on I could decide whether to tell the beasties or not. I counted the windows in the barracks, trying to remember which lights were on. I tried to figure out how far the machinery was from the barracks and in what position. And when we began to see the road, I worked that into the mental diagram, too.

Inside the fence, the men were not in such a hurry as they had been outside it. They were leaning against the barracks, sitting on stumps, smoking, talking. But there was still something edgy about them. They all turned to look at us curiously, as though strangers were an unusual and not necessarily welcome sight in here. "Just a couple of kids, lost in the woods," the guard kept explaining to them. Mostly the men smiled faintly and waved.

But there were a few whose faces were cold. One of them, holding a chain saw, said to the guard, "You forgot what happened at Coleville camp, and the others? You think the boss would like you taking those kids in here? They could have walked around outside."

"Two nice little kids? What harm can they do? Why not help them out?" another man said kindly. He stood out from the rest because he had long blond hair and a mustache.

The one who hadn't wanted us to come inside turned around and spat. He must be scared. Even inside the fence they all seemed a little scared, even the nice ones.

Exactly what had happened at the other camps?

ten

"You dope," Colette said icily when we were out on the road, the locked logging camp behind us. "I told you not to say anything. He almost didn't let us in."

I was glad I had disturbed her. "But nobody tells me anything," I complained. "Don't I deserve to know *something* about what's going on? I'm involved in this, too, now."

"Deserve? You're involved in this to save yourself—and the less you know, the safer you'll be. How many million times do I have to tell you that? If you ever see the family again, or the loggers, don't ask questions. Just keep quiet."

Around a bend, out of sight of the camp, Colette sat down by the side of the road, next to a flat rock. She got out her notebook and tore off a sheet of paper and handed it to me, along with a pen. "Draw the camp, as accurately as possible. Then we'll compare notes and make sure it's right and give it to them."

"And what are they going to do with it?"

She gave me her new cold, determined look. "Just help me as much as you can. If you can do that, then you might make it through this."

And so I sat there in the gathering darkness and the evening birdcalls, the rise and fall of the insect sounds, drawing a picture of the logging camp, putting in what I thought were the right distances. I did try to make it as accurate as possible. Not to help the beasties, but because I was scared of what they would do to me if I made a mistake.

And I kept thinking about what this must be for. Fingers had referred to the loggers as the enemy. She had said what they were doing was slaughter. And for the first time I wondered: What would happen to the beasties when the whole forest was gone?

We compared our maps, working quickly, because soon it would be too dark to see. We talked about where the different machinery was, and which barracks lights were on, and distances. And now, because I had been right earlier, Colette agreed that my observations were usually more accurate. "Maybe it's because you play baseball," she said wryly.

Then she went on quickly. "The guy who let us in, he left the rifle in the guardhouse, right?"

"He had it in there when we first saw him, and he didn't have it when he walked us through the camp," I said. "But he could have gone back and moved it somewhere else later."

"Well, it's still worth noting," she muttered.

We agreed on most things, for a change. And then Colette had me draw another map, as neatly as possible, including all the corrections we had made. I couldn't deny that it made me feel a little better that she let me draw the final version. At least I was better than her at *something*.

"Hey, how come we're supposed to label things in English?" I asked her as I handed her the map. "Only Fingers can speak English, and she can't see."

"She taught some of the others how to read certain English words, only the ones they needed to know."

"That must mean she used to be able to see," I said. "And how did she learn English anyway?"

Colette didn't answer me. "Okay. That's done," she said, sounding relieved. She stood up. "Now let's get this to them fast, while we can still see where we're going."

It wasn't too far to the driveway to our house. We kept away from the house and went into the woods behind. I followed her, making sure to notice and remember the specific trees we passed as we went. She pulled the trapdoor partly open and let my map flutter down into the darkness.

Colette couldn't seem to relax that evening.

"Why are you so fidgety, Colette?" Mom asked her several times.

"Fidgety?" Colette said, pretending to laugh. "I'm just . . . uh, excited about my book."

Mom gave Dad a significant look. But he wasn't paying much attention. "No *Aceropala* today," he complained. "What's happened to it all?"

When Mom was out of the room, Colette kept looking at her watch. Why did she care what time it was? What was she going to do? What were the beasties going to do, now that we had given them the information they wanted? I didn't try to get Colette alone and ask her, because I knew she wouldn't tell me.

And *because* she wouldn't tell me, I decided what *I* was going to do. I knew it wouldn't be easy, and I was really scared at the thought of doing it. But it was the only way I would get any answers. And after what we had done today, I needed some answers.

I made sure to be the last one to go to bed, and before I did, I turned on the kitchen light. I left the door of my bedroom slightly ajar, so that I could hear.

It was midnight when Colette crept out of her room. She was so quiet I could barely hear her, and I couldn't tell if she went out the front door or not.

I waited for fifteen minutes. Then, as quietly as possible, I slipped down the stairs and out the front door. I didn't turn on the flashlight until I got out in back of the house.

I was lucky. It was windier now; the trees were making a lot of noise, covering up the sound of my feet in the underbrush, in case anybody was listening. For a few minutes I was afraid I was lost, and panicked, but I kept looking back to the house, to the light in the kitchen window, and that guided me. Sooner than I wanted, my flashlight found the bare sapling that opened the trapdoor.

I hesitated. It still wasn't too late to turn back. If I did, I would very likely be safe from the beasties—I had done a good job on the map. But if I didn't go into the tunnels now, I would probably never know what was really going on.

I tried to tell myself that maybe they wouldn't mind if they found me down there on my own. After all, I had helped them. But somehow I knew they didn't want me around, especially not tonight. I was going to have to go down into their territory and try not to get caught. It wouldn't be easy; it probably wasn't even possible. But if I didn't try, I would never find anything out.

I opened the trapdoor a crack and shined the flashlight in—it was risky to use the flashlight at all, but here I had no choice. As soon as I saw that the platform was in place and the spikes were covered, I turned off the light and hid it in some underbrush. It was too dangerous to use it inside; I would have to feel my way in the darkness.

I didn't open the trapdoor completely; I didn't want the tunnels to be exposed tonight. I could worry about getting out later. It was a squeeze to get through the small hole, and it was even trickier getting through it without fully opening it. It was easy for the beasties because they were all so skinny, as though they never got enough to eat.

No, that was wrong. Not all the beasties were small and skinny. The Queen was bigger than Dad— too big to ever get through this trapdoor. She was also too big to enter the small upper tunnel that led to the trapdoor. Had the tunnels been designed on purpose so that the Queen could never get out?

I slithered through. The sound of my landing on the platform coincided with the sound of the trap-door slamming shut. I froze, my heart pounding, waiting in the blackness for sounds approaching. I made myself wait there for five minutes. And no-body came; nobody seemed to have heard. Whatever was happening must be going on in another part of the tunnels.

Bent over, I groped my way blindly through the still, stale-smelling hole. This tunnel was narrow enough that I could feel both sides with my hands, and that helped. I managed not to trip over any roots. Sooner than I expected, I came to the fork.

The right-hand fork, the one that led down to the council room and the dormitory, was completely dark and silent. But the left-hand fork, the one Co-lette and I had taken the first time we came down here, was more brightly lit than I had ever seen it. And there was a whirring noise coming from that direction that I had never heard down here before. I went that way.

A tiny lamp glowed on the floor in the room with the bicycle, and I could see and hear a young, large beastie furiously riding the bike, panting. I slipped past that doorway toward the next room, the operating room, from which a very bright light was coming. I stood at the edge of the doorway and peeked inside.

I went cold and sick all over.

Electric lights flickered brightly over the two operating tables. An old, small beastie stood between the tables. All I could see were its pale, fishy, wrinkled eyes. The rest of it was covered in white—white cap, white surgical mask, white gown, white gloves. Another small beastie stood behind, helping. Their garments were spattered with blood.

A large beastie with only one arm lay shirtless and unconscious on the nearer table. On the farther table, also shirtless and unconscious, lay a logger—the one with the long blond hair and mustache, who had spoken kindly to us that afternoon. The beastie in the middle was cutting very slowly and carefully into the logger's shoulder, concentrating hard. I remembered Fingers' anatomical references. The doctor beastie would have to be very delicate with all the muscles and tendons and nerves, so that it could attach the logger's arm to the beastie and it would work. Now it had reached the bone. The nurse handed the doctor a saw. I could hear the brittle, rasping sound of it.

I couldn't stand to watch, and I was afraid I'd make a retching noise and they'd notice me. I hurried off down the tunnel without thinking, continuing in the direction I'd been going, farther and farther away from the trapdoor.

We helped them, we helped them do this, I repeated over and over to myself in my head, groping my way down the tunnel. I kept going and going, following no plan, my mind a complete mess. I barely noticed that the tunnel eventually began sloping upward, getting narrower, the ceiling lower. I don't know how far I went before I began to hear the noises and stopped.

The noises were close. There was a dim light ahead around a corner, not bright like the electric one, and shadows were swelling and shrinking against the dirt wall. I crouched against the wall where I was in the darkness, trying to press myself into it, to be as invisible as possible.

The noises consisted of many footsteps ahead of me, no voices. But even without voices, there seemed to be more activity going on in here tonight than I had ever been aware of before. A small beastie ran right past me in the darkness, carrying some-thing, not seeming to notice me.

I was terrified, but at the same time also strangely numb from the hideous operation I had seen—maybe I was in shock. And so I dared to inch a little closer to the light. Where the tunnel turned, there was an indentation in the wall. I squeezed into it and was able to crane my neck just enough to see around the corner.

Moonlight silvered an open trapdoor in the ceil-ing. Big uniformed beasties came jumping lightly and quietly down through it. Some were carrying rifles, others chain saws, and others cardboard boxes, some of which I could see had cans in them. They handed them to the small beasties in loincloths waiting in-side and then climbed out again. This trapdoor was above a tunnel intersection, and luckily most of the small beasties went off with their burdens in the other direction, away from me, which seemed to slope down. The few who ran past me didn't seem to notice me—yet.

Colette, her hair pulled tightly back, stood off to the side. She held a flickering candle, shading it with her hand; she kept checking her watch. A large uni-formed beastie beside her was watching the activity and making notes on a clipboard.

Fingers was there, too, squatting in a corner, out

of the way, not doing anything but listening hard. I figured she must be useless on this mission because she couldn't see.

I crouched there, squeezed into the corner indentation in a kind of daze. I had some answers now. This trapdoor had to be right *inside* the logging camp we had spied on today, an entrance invisible and unknown to the loggers who worked there. The loggers thought their barbed wire fence would protect them, but the trapdoor was built within it. Now that Colette and I had told the beasties the exact layout of the camp, they could sneak up there in the middle of the night and work quickly, not having to waste time looking for things in the darkness—stealing weapons and provisions, stealing a logger's arm. And what about the big logging machinery, the location of which was so important for us to tell them? What were they doing to that?

I didn't know how long it had taken me to get here or how long I crouched there watching. Beasties were coming back inside and staying now, and there were fewer and fewer of them entering. Colette showed her watch to the beastie beside her, and then she and the beastie both looked up at the trapdoor. The beastie gestured at the trapdoor and whispered something, as if communicating with someone waiting outside.

Then I heard footsteps behind me. I scrunched back into the indentation, turning my feet to the side so that no one would trip over them. Two small beasties came trotting along, more slowly than the others, panting because of the long object they were carrying between them. They managed—just barely—to miss my feet. Then they were under the trapdoor, and I could see they were carrying the logger, strapped onto a kind of stretcher. He had a right arm and surgical dressing over his empty left shoulder.

Two large beasties reached down from outside the trapdoor while the large ones inside lifted the stretcher up to them. It was a struggle to get this full-grown adult on a stretcher through the small opening. The beasties pulled and shoved, twisting the stretcher one way and then another. Earth spilled down, and finally the stretcher was outside. The beasties up there ran off with it.

Colette and the beasties inside waited impatiently for the ones outside to take the logger wherever they were going to leave him. Colette kept looking at her watch, shifting from one foot to another. They must all be terrified that the beasties would be spotted out there.

But in a few minutes the beasties returned, handed the stretcher back down, and jumped down themselves. The last one grabbed the stool and climbed up and pulled the trapdoor quietly shut.

And then they were all embracing, even Colette. The mission had been a success. Because of Colette and me, they had been able to do it all quickly enough not to get caught.

Fingers gave an order, and a group of small beasties broke away and ran squeaking off, presumably to report the success of the mission to the rest of the colony. The others continued to embrace. It was awful to see Colette hugging these creatures with their identical fierce features and huge teeth.

The only one who was not embracing was Fingers. She had gotten to her feet, but she was not part of the joyous celebration; she was left out because she had no eyes. If she hadn't been so gross-looking, I might have felt a little sorry for her.

Still, Colette had told me Fingers was second in command. The Queen was too big to get this close to the surface, so now it was Fingers who was issuing the orders. The large beasties began to disperse in the other direction from me. Colette started after them.

"Wait, Colette. Something is not right," Fingers said in the sudden darkness. "There is a wrong smell, very close."

eleven

With Fingers gripping my right arm and another uniformed beastie gripping the other, they marched me down, down, deep into the tunnels.

Colette followed with her candle. Our shadows trembled ahead of us on the steeply sloping dirt floor. "Colette, help me! Tell them I just wanted—"

"Shut up!"

We stopped suddenly, and the beastie on my left bent over and tugged at something on the slanting floor, exposing a rectangle of blackness—an interior trapdoor. The beastie jumped down. Without a word, Fingers pushed me into the hole. I cried out as I slid through, landing painfully on my back. The beastie who had jumped through the trapdoor grabbed my left arm, and an instant later Fingers was squeezing my right elbow, pulling me roughly to my feet. There was a light thump, and the candle flickered back to life behind us.

I turned back as they tugged me forward. *"Please,* Colette! Tell them how much I helped with the map!"

She didn't answer. She pushed something on the wall, and a platform on the floor sprang open, exposing a pit full of sharpened stakes directly under the trapdoor we had just fallen through.

Fingers and the other beastie pulled me forward. I stumbled and almost fell again as we started down a flight of crude steps, earth packed with stone, very steep and uneven. Fingers and the other beastie were shorter than I, but they were strong, keeping me on my feet as we descended.

We reached a blank wall. Were they going to kill me here?

The beastie on my left kicked open another trapdoor. Fingers pushed me into it. I screamed, thinking of the stakes.

And landed on another platform. The others jumped down and grabbed me again. Here there were more steps, wider, winding. We passed an opening on the right, from which came the sound of lapping water. We continued down, turning.

Now there was light below us and chattering, squeaky voices. The steps ended on a paved floor.

This cavern was the largest I had been in and dazzlingly bright to my dark-adjusted eyes. Burlap curtains hung in some of the doorways, a luxury I hadn't seen in the tunnels before. Large beasties in uniform stood along the lamplit walls, holding rifles—the ones missing a leg had the rifles propped on crutches. They all turned instantly and stared at me with the same sharp, toothy, chinless face. At Fingers' orders, two of the small beasties in loincloths, both of them with no arms, quickly wobbled off and disappeared through a very wide curtain at the end of the hallway.

I coughed as we passed a smoky open doorway and a blast of heat—it looked like a kitchen in there. And then they pulled me abruptly to the left, through a curtain into a small chamber with a single lamp hanging from the center of the ceiling. A beastie with a rifle followed us.

Fingers gave an order. They pushed me to the

floor. The beastie who wasn't Fingers kept me there, its foot planted on my chest. The beastie with the rifle stood beside it, the rifle pointed at my head. Colette and Fingers moved to my other side.

I was gasping for breath. "Why are you doing this? I helped you. I drew the map. Colette, *tell them!*"

"No reason to talking now," Fingers said. "Save pretty lies for Queen."

"I'm not lying!"

Fingers shook her head. "Lying? True thing? You thinking Queen care? Queen care only about mating."

"Mating? But what does—"

Fingers gestured, and the beastie pushed its foot harder onto my chest. "Queen care about colony surviving. Queen not be happy you peeking and prying and interrupting pleasure and necessary of mating. Queen not be happy we must bringing you down into her special territory." Her voice dropped. "I feel you before, Doug brother—bone and tendon and sinew. I thinking Queen want more strong arm and leg for colony."

"No!" I screamed. "Can't you understand? I'm on your side!" That *was* a lie, for sure. But I'd say anything to get out of this.

And why wasn't Colette doing a single thing to help me? They *must* have brainwashed her.

All at once they stiffened to attention, even Colette. The gigantic Queen lumbered into the room, her voluminous red bathrobe-like garment trailing on the floor. Her face was flushed, her lipstick smeared. She took one look at me, then opened her mouth impossibly wide and bellowed. The others shrank away from her.

"Colette, *please!* Tell them I—"

But the Queen's voice was louder than mine. She was barking a harsh stream of syllables, looking from one to the other of them, shaking a red-nailed finger at me.

"Queen very angry at humans," Fingers told me in a quick whisper. "Say fault of humans her litter die. Want human die."

Then the Queen lurched toward Colette, towering over her, her deep voice rising to a shriek. Colette went very pale, and Fingers moved protectively closer to her. You didn't have to understand their language to know that the Queen was blaming Colette for my unwanted presence here. I would have enjoyed it if I hadn't been so scared—the little brat had done *nothing* to help me tonight.

There was a footstep in the doorway, and they all spun around as another beastie entered the room.

The Queen's expression instantly softened. This was the same beastie she had been flirting with at the conference. He was noticeably taller and stronger than any of the others except the Queen. Somehow I could tell he was male.

Why were he and the Queen the only ones in the entire colony with recognizable gender? I remembered Fingers saying, "Queen care only about mating."

Fingers was talking fast, explaining something to the Queen. The Queen turned reluctantly away from the tall beastie. But she wasn't listening to Fingers. She was looking carefully at me, her eyes roving over my limbs.

The Queen grunted and lifted her hand. Fingers' voice died. The Queen uttered a single syllable, a command. They all stared down at me.

"No," Colette said, as if she understood. "You . . . you can't."

The Queen hissed at her, and I could see the spray of saliva. Colette backed away. The Queen glared at her for a long moment.

Then the Queen lifted her head and patted her hair. She pressed her lips together, as if trying to fix her lipstick. She moved toward the male beastie in the doorway.

Unexpectedly, the Queen spun around. She

pointed at Fingers and uttered another command. Those who had watches looked at them quickly, then at me. The Queen turned away. She was smiling down at the male beastie as they left the room.

The others all turned to Fingers, looking grim. Fingers spoke. The beastie lifted its foot from my chest and gestured at me to stand up. I got to my feet, dazed. The other beastie was still pointing the rifle at me.

"Death sentence," Fingers said softly. "One half hour."

"No!" Colette said again, her features outlined with tension. "You can't. It will just—"

Fingers shushed her with a hand.

And suddenly my brain went into action—the same fight-or-flight adrenaline rush I had experienced when they kidnapped me. "Colette's right," I said, breathing hard. "If I don't go back, it will just make trouble for you. You don't think they'll look for me? You don't think they'll ask Colette? Anyway, how can I be a threat, with so many of you and only one of me—and a rifle pointed at my head?"

"Not threat here and now, very true thing," Fingers agreed, frowning, twisting her hands together. "But very massive and very dangerous threat if we ever ever risk to letting you up to the outside again."

"Tell them, Colette," I said, looking hard at her. "Tell them who knew the most direct way to the logging camp. Tell them who knew the right distances. Tell them who drew the map that made their mission a success—unless you were honest enough to tell them already."

"Doug's right," she said staunchly and stood up straighter. "It was Doug who knew the right distances. It was Doug who drew the map we gave you. There, uh, wasn't time for me to . . . tell all the details to you before."

Fingers looked back in my general direction, her head lifted slightly. "So Doug brother it is who have very strong, very accurate eyes." There was a definite tone of bitterness there, underneath the praise.

"And I didn't give anything away at the logging camp either, right, Colette?" I prodded her. "I could have. I'd been down in the tunnels already; I knew where they were. And I didn't give anything away. I did exactly what you asked me to do. If I'd given anything away, do you think the mission would have been a success? No way. So if you trusted me then, why can't you trust me now?"

"Because you sneaking and snooping down in our territories where we don't want you here!" Fingers said instantly. "Very risking and dangerous timing to come, in middle of important mission. Making trouble in time of hazard." She shook her head. "No. Cannot trust." She paused, looking implacable. "If human we cannot trust, can never letting it out of tunnels alive. Queen want you dead—one half hour."

"Believe me, Fingers, you can trust him," Colette said. "He's too much of a coward to come down here just out of curiosity. He *must* want to help."

"Go now, Colette," Fingers said. "Not good for you to be here at final interrogation. We must find out what he know, before . . ." She paused. "Signal housekeeper to bringing drink."

"But—"

"Go!" Fingers commanded her, and the one with the rifle pointed it at Colette.

Colette gave me a miserable glance, but she left.

Sweat trickled down my temples and my ribs. I was trembling. Was it really too late? Or was there some way I could get Fingers to trust me, to help me? I didn't know how to convince her that I'd never betray them—especially since I didn't know *myself* that I'd never betray them.

And even if I *could* convince Fingers to trust me, would she be able to disobey an order from the Queen?

But somehow my brain was still working. I remembered how Fingers looked while the mission was going on—how unhappy she was that she couldn't participate in it. I had an idea.

"You know what it feels like to want to be part of something and be left out for reasons you can't control?" I asked, looking directly at Fingers. She couldn't see, but maybe she could sense it somehow. "I drew the best map I could, and I wanted to do more. But how could I? Nobody would tell me anything. And I knew that if I didn't come down here and see for myself, I'd *never* find out." I spoke with more conviction now—what I was saying was at least partly true. "It was scary, I knew it was dangerous, but I couldn't keep away. I wanted to help, and I didn't know any other way to do it."

There was no change in Fingers' expression. I swallowed. "I . . . I didn't betray you before, and I never would. That's . . . all I can say."

Fingers didn't respond because at that moment a small beastie came in with a tray of their drinks, in clay mugs. It seemed to be the small beasties in loincloths who did the household tasks, the big beasties in uniforms who did the dangerous things. In the light here I could see not only the beating of the small beastie's heart through its thin skin, but also the shadows of its lungs and stomach.

Fingers and the other two beasties took mugs and gulped thirstily from them. The small beastie left.

They all drank this stuff, including Colette. Had this drink changed her from a precocious little girl into someone cold and determined? Whatever it was, I was glad they hadn't offered me any.

But while they were busy drinking, maybe I could distract Fingers, and make her think I cared about them. "What is your drink?" I asked hesitantly.

"We making from special fungus. Everything we do for ourselves here. Independent. Not depend for anything, anything, anything at your 'civilization.'" She said the word with contempt. "And still they come to making war on us. That is first question I ask. What I meaning when I say humans making war on us?"

I felt like asking her if she had put Colette through this that first night. But that wasn't the way to get her on my side. Anyway, her question was easy. I had noticed their warlike terminology at the conference—and both "missions" had been directed against the logging operation. "The humans are making war on you by cutting down the forest," I said.

"We living by ourselves, hurting no one," Fingers said slowly, not telling me if I had answered correctly or not. "And then, humans coming. Have very large, nasty weapons, very powerful, very brutality. We have nothing. Very difficult to trying and stop them. Next question: What humans are destroying?"

I hoped they would all be this easy. "The forest," I said.

"Not correct!" she said. "What humans are destroying when destroy forest? *Forest* more than just word to us."

This wasn't so easy after all. What was she getting at? "Uh . . . the forest," I said, feeling stupid— and terrified. This wasn't some quiz in school; my life really did depend on it. "The forest, it's, uh . . . where you live. It's what hides you, protects you. It's . . . your home!"

"Correct answer to first part of question," she said and took a swig of her drink. She smiled her terrible smile. "And now to answering second part. What *else* humans destroy when destroy forest?"

For a moment I was stumped. Then I thought of all the ecological stuff in school and on TV. "Changing the air. Changing the climate. Uh . . ." I remembered Colette's little speech at the dry streambed. "Destroying water and streams. Destroying other creatures that live in the forest too."

"That not answer I want," Fingers said, her

empty eye sockets fixed on me. I was aware of the two other beasties impatiently watching me too. Did they understand what we were saying?

It wasn't the best situation for thinking clearly. I looked away from Fingers' face, still a little sickened by it. The beasties wouldn't have been nearly as gross if so many of them hadn't been maimed. . . .

"I waiting," Fingers prodded me. "Half hour going fast."

Maimed . . . Why *were* so many of them maimed? Could that possibly have something to do with what she was asking me? I had wondered earlier if all the missing limbs and the Queen's litter dying could have any relation to their attacks on the logging camps. An answer occurred to me. It was crazy and farfetched; it was probably all wrong. Still, it might be better than *no* answer. And how could I make my situation any worse?

"When they destroy the forest, they're also destroying *you*. Your bodies, I mean."

Fingers leaned forward. "I hearing, but cannot believing. Is this truly *Doug* speaking?"

Was she praising me for what I had said, or was she angry? I couldn't tell. "I'm sorry if it's a dumb answer. And I don't understand how it would work, exactly, or if it's enough of an explanation. But you said the Queen was angry because it was the humans' fault her litter died. And what else did the humans do but cut down the trees? And you are so much a part of the forest, a *deep* part. So maybe when they cut down the trees, something else happens. And it's . . . it's cutting down your bodies too."

"Yes, that is what I am meaning!" she snapped at me and took another drink. With her free hand she touched the places where her eyes had been. "Before. Before they come with their big screaming machines. Tunnels are home, not hiding place, not prison. Many family, many different colony all in forest. Different family visiting together, not hiding apart, like now. Sunlight always too pain for us, but at night we can going outside, before they come—outside and clean air and big space and wind and rain . . ."

Her voice dropped. "Before they come, I have two good eyes." She quickly took another drink. "I am very strong one, good muscle, good brain, synapses and convolutions. I could being Queen some day, not just chief officer. Even I learning English, to be better leader. Then enemy begin slaughter of home. Special fungus for drink harder to find. Disease come. Our families starting to weaker. Losing arm, losing leg, Queen losing babies . . ."

Her voice faded. And I dared to ask, hoping to

sound sympathetic, "And that's why . . . why you lost your eyes?"

"No! Not why!" she said angrily. She touched her empty sockets again. "Some, like me, not getting disease. I am healthy one. But one night searching for fungus. And birds come. Big birds. Birds crazy, for losing their home. Birds attacking. Taking eyes. Even though I am not disease, still, have no eyes. And that mean, I . . . can never being Queen." She drained her cup.

We stood there in silence. She wasn't asking any more questions—in fact, she had started telling *me* things. What did that mean?

Now the other two beasties were really getting uncomfortable. One of them looked at its watch, then spoke to Fingers.

My time was up. Whatever the interrogation had been for, it hadn't helped me.

"*Please* don't do it!" I begged Fingers, my voice cracking. "I answered your questions right. I want to help you. I—"

She lifted her hand in a gesture so sharp and so assured that my voice died. She issued orders to the other two beasties.

They stared at her, stunned, their mouths dropping open. They turned and looked at one another, then back to Fingers. They seemed frightened by whatever she had said to them.

Now Fingers was talking fast. She pointed out toward the corridor, put her hands over her stomach, then made a gesture of disapproval.

One of the other beasties started to argue with her. Fingers argued back, and hissed, and made a threatening gesture, rising up on her toes to make herself taller.

The two beasties seemed cowed now. They looked at each other again, then nodded unhappily at Fingers.

"Good. They will coming part of the way up with us, so others not having suspicion. They will not telling others what I am do. They know to trust me."

My heart began to pound. "What . . . what are you doing?"

She smiled—and somehow her face wasn't ugly anymore. "Do not have eyes, but have good smelling, and other sensing too. Maybe I know you a little now, Doug brother." The way she said my name wasn't sarcastic anymore; it was almost affectionate. "Coward, yes, to letting Colette coming here alone first night. But tonight you come, even though very coward. Make me think you care. And you knowing answer to very important questions—most humans cannot understand. Make me to trust—even though *you* not sure." She was still smiling, a very warm smile I had never seen on her face before. "Queen order me to killing you, Doug brother. But Queen not thinking very good this time now, too angry. I thinking clear. I thinking colony need you, same Colette. Time you to going home."

"You really mean it?" I said, my heart still pounding. I felt like crying now, crying because she was putting so much trust in me, disobeying the Queen, saving my life. "Gee, thanks," I said. It wasn't enough; there were no words deep enough to express my gratitude.

Colette was waiting outside the curtain. The other two beasties came part of the way with us. Fingers took us the final stretch up to the trapdoor. She embraced Colette and shook my hand. We stumbled home silently through the trees, too exhausted to talk. I still had many questions, but I couldn't think about them now. I was asleep before my head hit the pillow.

I was awakened much too soon by a knock at my door. "Huh?" I said.

"It's me," Mom said. "Can I come in?"

"Sure."

She stepped into the room and closed the door behind her. She seemed uncomfortable. "What have you and Colette been up to, Doug?" she asked me. "I've been noticing things."

"Things?" I said groggily.

"And now there are some men downstairs who insist on seeing you two. They say it's urgent. They won't tell me what it's about, but they look . . . grim."

"Who'd want to see us?" I said, not scared because I was still half asleep. "Who are they?"

"They're from the logging camp down the road."

twelve

Why would they be here if they didn't think we had something to do with the raid on the camp last night?

On the way down I whispered, "Colette, maybe you should do the talking. You're better than I am. And you're always telling me to keep quiet anyway."

But Colette didn't have her usual self-possession and confidence. She seemed as nervous as I was. "Maybe you could back me up, Doug," she said. "It was pretty impressive the way you proved yourself last night, answering Fingers' questions. I was listening at the curtain. I could hardly believe it."

And I could hardly believe she was complimenting me—and *relying* on me.

Her voice dropped. "But remember, if they ask you things directly, *do not* give anything away, not a hint. It would be a total disaster if the loggers got the faintest idea the tunnels even exist. There aren't many of the families left anymore."

Three men sat in the living room, each with a different kind of unpleasant expression on his face. One of them I recognized right away as the guard who had let us into the camp yesterday. The second one looked vaguely familiar; he might be another logger, maybe even the one who had spat on the ground because he didn't want us inside. The third man was unfamiliar, old and fat. He was the only one wearing a suit; the others wore jeans and flannel shirts and boots.

Dad wasn't anywhere around. He must be out looking for his fungus, so he wouldn't be here to defend or protect us. Mom seemed confused. Mrs. Sloan, in her mask, was dusting in the dining room, right across from the living room, obviously curious and wanting to hear everything that went on.

"These are the children?" the man in the suit said when we entered the room.

"Yeah, that's them," the guard said. He sighed and looked glumly at us.

Colette did her best to smile at the guard. "Oh, hi," she said in the childish, innocent voice she could so easily put on. "Thank you again for helping us find our way yesterday." She turned to Mom. "We got lost in the woods and this man at the logging camp helped us get home," she explained. She pushed her hair out of her eyes—she was wearing it down today to seem more babyish—and looked back at the guard with a cute, questioning expression on her little round face.

"You don't know what happened last night?" the guard asked.

"What happened last night—after you two got in and checked out the place," the logger said, and when I heard his voice, I knew he was the one who had mentioned the boss yesterday and spat. I figured the old guy in the suit must be the boss. I felt the beginnings of panic.

"Last night?" Colette said, looking confused. "What happened last night?"

"My business just down the road was thoroughly and brutally vandalized and burglarized to the extent that we're going to have to shut down operations for

I don't know how long," said the boss. And then he just stared at us, touching his fingers together, one leg crossed over the other.

"Oh, how awful!" Mom said and sank into a chair. "That's frightening, something like that so close to us." Then she stopped for a moment. She did a kind of double-take reaction. "Wait a minute. Did you come here to suggest that Doug and Colette might have something to do with it?" she accused them, sounding angry now.

"What we're saying, *ma'am*," the boss said, "is that late yesterday afternoon your kids came out of the forest, told my guard they were lost, and persuaded him to let them come through the camp. I have strict rules about not letting anybody in without ID, but my guard made the mistake of feeling sorry for them."

The boss gave the guard a look. The guard couldn't meet his eye. He was clearly in big trouble.

The boss continued. "My guard tells me both children carefully watched him unlock the gate, which is a complicated process, and your son here asked him about security. Then my guard walked the children all the way across the camp. They could see where all the different equipment was, which barracks were occupied, all that stuff."

The boss paused and cleared his throat, looking

at Mom, not us. "Then, last night," he went on slowly, his head tilted to the side, his fingers still pressed together, "what must have been practically an army of vandals got inside the camp. How'd they get in? They went directly to all the equipment and either stole or trashed it. Sugar in the gas tanks of all the vehicles; they're ruined now. How did they do it so fast if they didn't already know exactly where all the equipment was? They went right to the occupied barracks and gratuitously mutilated one of our men. They did all of this in what must have been a remarkably short period of time, because the night guard in the gatehouse—not this one, he does the day shift—was not even aware of what was going on until it was all over. How did they know exactly where my men had left the equipment? And isn't it interesting that it happened the very same night after your kids were inside the camp—the *only* outsiders to enter the camp in seven months?"

"Well, it's obviously just a coincidence," Mom said hotly. "What possible connection could my kids have to a gang of vandals? I mean, my kids aren't like that; they're not juvenile delinquents. Anyway, we've only been here for a few days."

"Yeah," Colette said. "And Mom, what he's not telling you is that something like this has been happening around here at other logging camps that Doug and I never got close to. Doug asked the guard if all logging camps had this much security, and he said around here they do, because of what happened at the other camps." Then she added, to the boss, "Isn't that right, sir?"

"That's what my guard said, too, trying to defend you kids—and himself," the boss said, giving the guard another sour look.

Colette and I glanced at each other. Of course, by defending us, the guard was also defending himself for letting us in. Still, he didn't seem angry at us, even now, when he was in trouble. He really was as nice a guy as he had come across as yesterday.

"And maybe that argument would have worked," the boss continued, "until we found this."

He took a folded piece of notebook paper out of the pocket of his suit jacket. I felt the panic growing. He flattened the paper out on the arm of his chair. "A detailed map of the camp, with estimated distances and everything labeled in neat—but not adult—hand-writing. We found it next to a ruined piece of equipment in the camp this morning. Might be interesting to do a little handwriting test and see how each of your kids writes the word *barracks*, for instance."

How could the beasties have been so stupid, leaving my map behind in the camp?

Then I felt a cold pang in my stomach. Maybe it *hadn't* been a mistake—the beasties were very methodical and well organized. Maybe they had left my map in the camp on purpose, for the loggers to find. Then the loggers would believe humans were behind the raid, not something from the forest. The blame for the terrible things the beasties had done would be shifted from them—onto me.

And it was Colette who had forced *me* to draw the map for her precious beasties. Maybe she had known all along that they were going to do this, to incriminate me and protect themselves.

"That ruined equipment is worth thousands and thousands," the boss said. His voice was still calm, but his face was a little red now. Clearly he was more concerned about the equipment than the logger losing his arm. "There are institutions for children who are proven to be involved in crimes of this magnitude. And handwriting samples are *very* definitive proof in a court of law."

I was sweating now, and my mouth was dry. This guy was the boss. He owned the camp. He had money and power, and that's what made you win in court. And he was talking about reform school. Colette might be too young, but I wasn't—and it was *my* handwriting on the map. But it was really all Colette's fault—hers and the beasties'.

Sure, I had felt sorry for them last night when I learned what was happening to them. And I had been so grateful to Fingers for letting me live, against the Queen's orders. But the beasties hadn't told me beforehand *why* they wanted me to draw a map of the logging camp. They had tricked and scared me into doing it. Was I ready to go to reform school to protect them? Not very likely.

"Of course, if the children could help us, if they could tell us exactly who *did* vandalize the camp and how, then all charges would be dropped," the boss said, his lower jaw jutting forward as he stared hard at Colette and me.

I couldn't help it. I turned and looked at Colette, terrified. She was still in control, still steadfast, looking at the boss with an expression of innocent bewilderment. "Vandalize the camp?" she said. "How awful! Why would anybody *do* something like that?"

But her innocent act wouldn't work. As soon as they compared my handwriting to the handwriting on the map, they would know I had drawn it. And if we didn't tell them about the beasties, then *I* was the one who would have to go to reform school.

Why should I make that kind of sacrifice for the beasties and their forest? Some people might do it; Colette might do it. But it wasn't the kind of thing I could do, no matter what I had told them last night when I was trying to save my life. I wasn't that kind of hero.

Hero? I wasn't that brainwashed yet. Would it be heroic to side with those nonhuman creatures—with their strange animalistic society I didn't really understand—against other human beings? What did I owe the lying, tricking beasties anyway? The only explanation Fingers had given me for their brutal destruction of the camp was that hurting the forest hurt them, and what did that really mean?

Even if it was true, the loggers didn't know about it. The beasties were attacking them for a supposed crime they didn't even know they were committing. And they wanted me to go to reform school for them.

Colette would hate me; the beasties would hate me. But I could take their hatred. Reform school I couldn't take.

"Let me see that paper. I can recognize my own kids' handwriting," Mom said, starting to get up.

"Wait!" I said.

Mom sat down. Everyone was staring at me. Colette's eyes actually seemed to flash at me in fury and warning. But she wasn't the one who would be going to reform school.

I thought of Fingers losing her eyes, and how thin and weak all the beasties were, and the Queen's litter dying. I thought of the ugly field of stumps and the stumps on the beasties.

And then I blocked out the thoughts. I was panting, as though I had just run around a baseball diamond. "It was . . ." I said. "It was—"

"The beasties," a voice said behind me.

Everyone turned and looked. Mrs. Sloan, who had obviously been listening just outside the door, had stepped into the room. She touched her mask. "It was the beasties who took my nose and the beasties who attacked your camp," she said to the boss and the guard and the logger. "It's not these children's fault. It was the beasties."

"Mrs. Sloan!" Mom said, startled. "What are you talking about?"

"They live in tunnels in the forest," Mrs. Sloan said. "They tricked me. They made me think I wanted to help them." She put her hand to her eyes; she was crying under her mask. "They got me down underground. I was working at the Coleville camp then, cooking. Remember what happened there?"

"Coleville filed for bankruptcy months ago," the boss murmured. "After his camp was wrecked."

"*Beasties?*" the logger said, trying to be sarcastic. "That's a word we joke about." But he sounded scared.

"Is this a joke?" Mrs. Sloan demanded, her voice catching, and pulled up her mask. There was a rough mass of purple scar tissue and two ragged punctures where her nose used to be. "And to think I *gave* it to them!" Tears were streaming down her face. "These babies are lucky they're still whole! I don't care what I promised the beasties. I can't let it happen again."

Mom gasped and turned her head away. Yesterday I would have been sickened by Mrs. Sloan's face, too. Now I was used to seeing such wounds. I thought, a missing nose? That's nothing.

And that's when it hit me. Okay, the beasties had taken an arm from the blond logger, the one who had spoken kindly to us. *But why hadn't they taken more?* There were many beasties who needed body parts, beasties who needed ears and hands and legs. Fingers needed eyes. And last night the beasties had the blond logger in the operating room—a strong, healthy man, full of body parts they desperately needed. And all they had taken was one arm.

It wasn't to be cautious that they had only taken

his arm. What they had done to the camp wasn't cautious. There could be only one reason they hadn't cut him to pieces and taken everything and left him dead: They cared. Absurd as it seemed, they were humane. I thought of how carefully they had brought the blond logger back up into the camp, risking being caught. They cared about him.

Yes, he was handicapped; he probably couldn't work as a logger now. But he was still alive, almost whole. He could function; he could take care of himself somehow. They had left him with a chance for some kind of a life, instead of taking everything from him—everything they needed because of what the logging companies were doing to the forest.

"The men talk about these—what is it?—*beasties!*" the boss asked the other two men.

"Yeah, it's a joke, sort of," the guard said, his eyes carefully avoiding Mrs. Sloan. "But we all know there's something out there. Something weird. You know it, too."

"You really believe these creatures are responsible for all the trouble around here?" the boss said, his skepticism beginning to dissolve.

"And now we're on the track of them," the logger said. "Where are they?" he asked Mrs. Sloan, also not looking at her. "How do we find them?"

And another thing I was thinking, as all this was going on. Colette and I had been down in their tunnels many times, at their mercy. And they hadn't taken anything from us. Why? The only answer there could be was that they cared about us, too. Even in their desperate situation, they were decent. They weren't monstrous. Yes, they mutilated some people. But not enough to ruin their lives. They were kind to their victims, at their own expense.

Mrs. Sloan snapped her mask back in place, to the relief of all the adults in the room. "I know where the entrance is—the entrance to their tunnels," she said. "It's in the forest, a place about twenty miles down the road, near the Coleville camp. Get some other men. I'll show you where."

"Right on," the logger said, jumping out of his chair.

"Just a minute," the boss said, lifting his hand. He turned to Colette and me. "There must be someplace closer to find these . . . beasties. Someplace these kids could easily get to. Someplace these kids could show us if they want to stay out of court. The map is evidence of their collusion with them."

But now I was sure the beasties couldn't have left the map there on purpose to set me up. That didn't make sense; I had only thought of it because I was so scared. The map would just be a prod to make me more likely to tell people about them. Leaving it there had to be a mistake.

And there was something a lot more important. A few minutes ago I had dismissed Fingers saving my life. Now that I had almost given them away, I realized what a great risk Fingers had taken—a risk for the entire colony. What she had done for me took on a lot deeper meaning.

"Beasties?" I said, before Colette had the chance. "We don't know anything about any beasties."

"It sounds like a silly story to me," Colette said.

"Leave the children out of it," Mrs. Sloan said to the boss. "I can show you how to find the beasties, believe me. Do you want to see the proof of it again?"

"No, thanks," the boss said, getting heavily to his feet. "Well, I guess we can't lose anything by going with her."

"You really believe her crazy story?" I said.

"I'm sorry, Mrs. Sloan," Colette said, "but I think you were having a hallu . . . hallucination or something."

"Get some other men," Mrs. Sloan said.

"We sure will," the logger said. "Let's move."

Mrs. Sloan and the two loggers were on their way

out. The boss followed them. But before he left, he turned back to us. "I'll get you if you had anything to do with this," he said. And then he waddled out the door.

In his haste, he had left the map on the arm of his chair.

thirteen

Colette raced to the chair and grabbed the map.

"Will you please tell me what is going *on?*" Mom demanded. Outside we heard engines starting up. Now that the others were gone, Mom was angry at us.

"The logging camps are having some kind of problem, I guess," Colette said and shrugged, holding the map in her hand. "We don't know any more about it than you do, Mom. Doug and I have to go now. We'll be right back."

"Now you wait just a minute," Mom said. She marched over to Colette, her hand outstretched. "Let me see that."

"It's nothing," Colette said, holding the map behind her back. "Couldn't you tell that boss was a cesspool?"

"Give it to me," Mom said.

"But we don't have time to—"

"Give it to me."

Colette handed it to her. What else could she do? Mom studied the map. She looked at me. "This *is* your handwriting, Doug!" she said, looking stunned.

"So I drew a map," I said. "It was just a game. We don't have time to talk about it now."

"That's right, Mom," Colette said, as if she were talking to a child. "Now just give it to me. We'll be back in a little while."

"You were at the logging camp yesterday. And you drew this map. And last night . . ." Now her voice was rising. "I knew something was going on. Did you two have anything to do with what happened at that logging camp?"

"Why *would* we, Mom?" Colette said, squeezing her hands together. She was bursting with impatience, and so was I. The beasties had to be warned that another system of the tunnels was about to be attacked. And we had to do it without giving anything away to Mom.

"Come on, Mom," I pleaded with her. "You know us. We're not vandals; we're not gang members. Why would we be involved in what happened at that camp? Do you really believe we were?"

"Well . . . no," she admitted.

"But that map could still get us in trouble," I said. "Give it back, please, and we'll get rid of it. Then the boss can't use it against us. I mean, do you *want* him to take us to court?" I was struggling for good arguments. "Think how expensive it would be. And that map is the only evidence. We'll just get rid of it and come right back."

Mom was bewildered as well as angry now. "I don't understand any of this," she said. "And what's all this business about . . . beasties, or whatever? And Mrs. Sloan's nose?"

"She's crazy," Colette said. "I tried to tell her. Something happened to her nose, and it made her crazy; she has these . . . hallucinations about it or something. Now please just give us the map so we can—"

The door slammed. "What were those people doing here?" Dad said, coming into the room with his specimen collection basket on his arm. "They were coming out of the driveway, going like crazy."

Mom turned to him, distracted. "It's all so *peculiar*," she began. "The logging camp down the road was vandalized. And they said—"

Colette grabbed the map out of her hand and headed for the door. I was right behind her.

"Where are you going? Come back here!" Mom shouted at us.

"Don't worry! Stay here! We'll be right back!" Colette called out.

"What are you so upset about?" we could hear Dad saying to Mom as we dashed across the porch. Maybe he would ask her questions and that would delay them, or maybe they wouldn't even follow us. We headed into the trees. They didn't seem to be following us. But once we had gotten far enough into the trees, Colette stopped to make sure they weren't behind us; the last thing we wanted was to lead them to the trapdoor.

They weren't anywhere in sight. Colette squatted and set the map on a bare patch of ground. She pulled a box of matches out of her pocket—probably the same ones she had used for the candle the night before—and set the map ablaze. It burned quickly. When the flames died, she dug a little hole with her hands and carefully buried the ashes. It was a relief that the map was destroyed, but that didn't stop me from worrying about everything else.

We raced to the trapdoor. I pulled it open; in the daylight I could see that the platform was safely covering the stakes. We checked again to make sure Mom and Dad were nowhere around, and then Colette jumped in and I squeezed through, letting the trapdoor slam shut above me.

"Alarm! Alarm!" Colette called out, small and adept enough to hurry ahead of me into the stale darkness. I felt my way with my right hand on the wall, bent over. We hadn't had a chance to bring the flashlight, but even I knew the tunnels better now. "Alarm!" I called out, too. We took the right fork, the one that led down to the council chamber and the dormitories. "Alarm!" we both called out again.

We began to hear scurrying and scuffling and then a voice, immediately ahead of us. "What is happen?" Fingers said.

"People from the logging camp," Colette told her, gasping. "Somebody left the map we gave you at the logging camp. They found it and came to our house. Did somebody leave it up there on purpose to get us in trouble?"

"No! Not in plan!" Fingers sounded frightened and angry. "I will find out who making such disorderly mistake and I will—"

"Don't worry about that now—we destroyed the map," Colette interrupted her. "And we acted dumb with the loggers. But Mrs. Sloan told them. She's taking them to some other tunnel entrance."

"Mrs. Sloan?" Fingers questioned.

"She works at our house," I said. "She gave her nose to some other colony. She's taking the men to a tunnel entrance about twenty miles away by road. Near the . . . what was the name, Colette?"

"Near the Coleville camp," Colette said. "Men are about to invade the tunnels near the Coleville camp."

"The family over there is very stupid," Fingers said, and hissed. "They trust adult humans. Come. This way."

Little lamps flickered ahead of us now, carried by small beasties. We hurried after them into the council room, which was already filling up quickly with big uniformed beasties.

The hulking Queen entered, rubbing her eyes, looking even older without her makeup. I crouched down behind Colette, hoping the Queen wouldn't see me.

Fingers spoke briefly to the whole group. The Queen rasped some questions, Fingers answered, and then the Queen was giving orders. Suddenly all the beasties were running out into the tunnels, going in different directions. We went with Fingers and some others back up the way we had come. "What were you saying?" I asked her.

"I tell them good thing I let you live, because you and Colette tell us other tunnels being invaded through trapdoor twenty-two. I tell them we must warn the family there—and then go to helping them repel the enemy."

"Can the enemy get . . . to this section?" I asked.

"We never go to those tunnels. Easy to close off, so they will never finding way here. Some stay here and make sure. Others go to helping the other family. Now, to alarm station."

At the fork I followed them around into the other tunnel. By the time I got to the rooms, somebody was already riding the bicycle, and the operating room was brightly lit. A beastie switched on a funny-looking, old-fashioned device in one corner, which I hadn't noticed before. There was a button on it, which beeped as the beastie rhythmically pressed it.

"What is that?" I asked Fingers.

"Machine to communicating over distance. Talk in code. Tell them humans coming."

"And then . . . they'll open the platform under their trapdoor?" I asked softly.

"Exactly," said Fingers, and smiled.

I wondered who would be the first man in, the

one who would be most deeply impaled on the sharpened stakes. It wouldn't be the boss, of course; he wouldn't enter the tunnels at all, I was sure. I just hoped it wouldn't be the guard who had helped us. Maybe the trapdoor would be too small for him to get through.

"Your parent," Fingers was asking us. "How much they hearing? How much they knowing?"

"Mom heard Mrs. Sloan talk about you," Colette said. "She called you by the bad name. But she doesn't know anything about the tunnels here or your trapdoor."

"I know you wanting to stay and help." Fingers reached out, her head tilted upward, and found each of our shoulders with one hand. "But I afraid your parent will be to wondering about you now. If you don't going back, maybe they try to searching for you, maybe tell others you missing. You did very good thing to warning us. But now, safer for us if you go to home. Best way to helping, go home now. Come back tonight, when parent sleep."

"But . . ." Colette protested.

"I speak true thing," Fingers insisted.

Even I was reluctant to leave. I didn't understand it, but I wasn't afraid of the battle. I wanted to help the beasties protect their territories. Still, neither of us could deny that what Fingers was saying made sense.

"Be careful the way you coming in tonight," Fingers warned us at the trapdoor. "We will opening the platform here for big security because is trouble. I thinking best to using the other entrance, from the house. We will leaving open for you."

"Okay," Colette said. We climbed out.

Dad was still asking Mom questions when we got back. That was probably why they hadn't followed us. Not having been there with the loggers and the boss and Mrs. Sloan, Dad did not feel the urgency that Mom did. And we had only been gone a very short time.

"Where were you?" Mom wanted to know.

"We just went to destroy the map," Colette said. It was a lame excuse; we could have destroyed it at home. But she had to tell Mom *something*.

"But I don't understand why you drew the map in the first place, Doug, or why the two of you had to go through the logging camp at all."

"Just what we said," Colette told her. "We got lost, and that guard showed us the way. It was quicker to go through the camp than to go all the way around, and it was starting to get dark. We were a little scared." She blinked at Mom and adjusted her glasses. "Then, afterward, when we knew where we were, we just thought it would be interesting to draw a map of the camp. If we were doing it for a bad reason, if we were helping somebody attack the camp, why would we leave the map lying around for the loggers to find? I guess the wind must have blown it back inside the camp or something. Anyway, it was just a coincidence that the vandalism happened last night."

"It's been happening all around here to logging camps," I said. "Didn't you hear anything about it when you were checking this place out, Dad?"

He thought for a moment. "Well, I seem to remember a couple of people making reference to some sort of troubles. And no one explained why the people who were living in this house left so quickly. They were very secretive about it all." He shrugged. "I didn't really pay much attention. I was thinking about my work."

"And I thought it would be so tranquil and idyllic and *safe* out here," Mom said, sighing. "And now *this*."

"Come on, it'll blow over," Dad said. He looked back at his nearly empty specimen basket. "Why can't I find any *Aceropala*?" he complained.

"But what was Mrs. Sloan talking about?" Mom asked. "Beasties? Weird creatures living in the forest? I don't understand."

"She's nuts," Colette said with complete conviction. "Losing her nose must have done something to her brain. We go out in the woods all the time. Okay, maybe there's some wild animals around; maybe that's what happened to her nose. But we haven't run into a *hint* of anything crazy like she was talking about."

"Well, I don't think I want her working here anymore if she has delusions like that," Mom said. "And the ugly way she exposed her wound to everybody!" She shuddered. "And she just ran right out of here in the middle of the day, leading those men out into the forest somewhere. That isn't what we're paying her for. I'd rather have somebody who's more responsible."

I didn't think she had to worry about Mrs. Sloan working here after today. I was pretty sure Mrs. Sloan wouldn't be back.

"And I don't want you kids going very deep into the forest anymore," Mom said. "Something's happened to you; I can feel it. Don't get out of sight of the house. And stay away from logging camps. I don't want you getting near any places where there might be trouble."

"Aren't you being a little overprotective?" Dad asked her, poking with irritation through his meager specimens. "Has all the *Aceropala* gone underground, or what? I didn't expect the logging would *already* . . . oh." He looked up at Mom. "Anyway, one of the reasons for coming here was so the kids could experience the wilderness, go on hikes, things like that, right? And if you don't want Mrs. Sloan working for us, it's not going to be easy finding somebody else. I thought you wanted to paint, not do housework."

While they were discussing this, Colette and I quietly left the room. She got her book and sat outside reading. I pretended to study, keeping away from Mom and Dad. Whenever I happened to glance out at Colette, she didn't seem to be concentrating very hard on her book.

It was horribly frustrating to know that somewhere, miles away through the tunnels, a battle was going on, and there was nothing we could do to help. How could either of us think about anything else? And it would have to be a very terrible battle: The beasties couldn't let any men who entered the tunnels go out alive.

But apparently Mrs. Sloan had gone into the tunnels and come out alive. She said she had been a cook at the Coleville camp before it shut down. Fingers had said the beasties in that area trusted human adults. Had those beasties made some kind of arrangement with Mrs. Sloan, similar to what had gone on between us and the beasties here? They must have convinced her to feel sorry for them, gotten her on their side. After all, she said she had *given* them her nose. And maybe she had told them the layout of the Coleville camp so they could attack it easily, just as we had helped our beasties attack the camp next to us.

And now Mrs. Sloan was showing the logging boss and his men her beasties' secret home. It was driving me crazy thinking about it. The day went on forever.

I lay down for a while in the afternoon, trying to get some rest. I hadn't had much sleep last night, and I probably wouldn't get any tonight. But I was too nervous to be able to sleep now.

Since we'd come to the country, Mom and Dad had gotten into the habit of going to bed early and getting up early. That was an advantage for us. Still, the evening was a long one.

And we knew we'd have to be especially careful sneaking out of our rooms tonight. Mom hadn't stopped worrying about what the loggers and Mrs. Sloan had said. I noticed her watching Colette when she thought I wasn't looking and watching me, too.

A couple of times I came upon Mom and Dad whispering together; they stopped as soon as they saw me. They were aware now that something strange might be going on. Mom especially would be on her guard tonight, listening for unusual noises. And so, even though everyone went to bed around ten-thirty, Colette and I waited until midnight, as we had agreed beforehand, to be sure Mom and Dad would be asleep.

Rain was pattering against my windowpane when I got up. Before I left my room, I arranged some pillows under the blanket so that it might just possibly look like I was in bed in case Mom checked. I knew Colette was doing the same thing.

We had synchronized our watches, and Colette was just stepping out of her room as I came out of mine. She had been reading; I had been lying in bed with the lights off for an hour and a half, so my eyes were much better adjusted to the darkness. I took her hand and led her very slowly down the hallway. The rain hammering on the roof helped to cover the sound of our footsteps. But just as we passed the door to Mom and Dad's room, a board creaked. We froze, waiting. There was no sound from their room, and we moved on.

The stairs were worse. Every step seemed to

creak. I was gritting my teeth. But we kept going, trying to make as little noise as possible.

Just as we reached the basement door, we heard what might have been a footstep upstairs. We very, very slowly pulled open the door and slipped through. We crept down the basement stairs. Colette could see better now. She went directly to the big old furnace and then around it to a tiny little space behind. I could barely squeeze in, the space was so small.

"It's too small for adult humans on purpose," Colette said. "I hope you can make it through."

She felt along the cement block wall with both hands until she found the right place and pushed. A section of four cement blocks swung away. Colette crawled through easily. For me it was a very tight squeeze; I scraped my stomach badly on the cement. Once inside, we could see by the little light coming from the basement that the four cement blocks were only a facade, about half an inch thick. They were attached to a wooden panel on this side. Colette pushed carefully until it clicked shut and then tightly fastened the latch on this side, doing it by feel. Now there was no light at all, and even with our adjusted eyes we could not see.

"How did you know where this was?" I asked her.

"They took me here the first night and showed me how it worked, in case I ever might need it. I was only here once. But I think I remember there's just one little tunnel that goes all the way straight back to near the trap door."

We had not brought the flashlight on purpose, feeling it would attract too much attention, trusting our own knowledge of the tunnels and the lights the beasties had.

"We have to crawl for a while," Colette said. "Come on."

I had never been in any part of the tunnels as small as this. Even squirming along on my belly, I could feel the walls and ceiling pressing against me. No adult could have gotten through here, and I almost couldn't myself. We kept inching along.

"What if Mom wakes up and finds we're not there?" I wondered, breathing heavily. "You think she'll call the cops or the state troopers or something?"

"I don't know. Maybe. But the only thing that matters is that they don't find these tunnels, and I don't see how they can."

How long was this going to go on? It was fifty-three yards from the back of the house to the trap-door in the woods. Were we going to have to crawl all that distance? I didn't ask Colette; I didn't want her to think I was complaining.

I knew I didn't have to be here. I also knew I couldn't stay away. Somehow I had already decided that I was on the side of the beasties and against the humans. And no matter what terrible things the beasties might have done to the loggers today, it was too late for me to switch sides now. I reminded myself that it was the humans who had done the attacking from the beginning; the beasties were just protecting themselves, struggling to survive.

I thought about how the logging boss had threatened and tried to bribe us—and how Fingers had taken the tremendous risk of saving my life. Maybe *that* was why I had decided to be on their side.

Finally we reached a place where the tunnel was big enough for me to get onto my hands and knees. Soon after that Colette said, "Okay, maybe you can stand up here." I couldn't exactly stand, but I could crouch, bent double at the waist.

Colette could stand, feeling her way with her hands. The tunnel turned sharply. And then we stepped out into the relative brightness and spaciousness of the area just under the trapdoor. As Fingers had warned us, the platform was upraised. In the light from around the edges of the trapdoor we could clearly see the sharpened stakes.

I was glad there were no impaled bodies under this trapdoor.

The light was even brighter when we reached the fork, coming from the left-hand tunnel, where the operating room was. I was not eager to see what might be going on in the operating room tonight, and I didn't think Colette was either. And there were lots of sounds now coming from the other direction, the tunnel that led down to the council chamber and dormitories. We went that way.

We followed the noises of voices and footsteps down, down, past the council chamber and the dormitory rooms. From the sound of it, there were a lot of beasties around. Soon we would know what had happened when the loggers had invaded that afternoon. I was desperate to find out—but also scared of the answer.

Light coming from a doorway beyond the dormitory brightened the tunnel. We could see that there was fresh mud on the tunnel floor, with many footprints in it, and a lot of debris scattered around. I realized now that the tunnels had always before been swept clean.

We looked inside the door. I heard Colette's sharp intake of breath. I must have made a noise, too.

It was a large room, with no furniture, and crowded. Many beasties sat huddled on the floor, possessions gathered around them. They looked like refugees.

fourteen

These new beasties were clearly the same species as the ones we were friends with. They had the same matted hair, nearly transparent skin, big eyes, and extra teeth. Many of them were missing limbs. Like our beasties, they all shared the same face.

But it was a different face from the one we knew.

Our beasties had narrow features, high cheek-bones, sharp noses, and almost no chin. The new beasties had round cheeks, pug noses, and long chins that protruded out from underneath their lower lips. The difference was very striking—and unsettling.

"Of course," Colette breathed. "They have a different Queen."

"Huh?" I said. I knew somehow I understood what she was talking about, but at the moment her meaning eluded me.

She gripped my arm. "Where's Fingers? Can you see her?"

"No."

"We've got to find her. Come on." She stepped into the room.

I heard a sudden scuffling and loud hissing somewhere behind me. I didn't look; I quickly followed Colette into the room.

The new beasties had to be from the Coleville tunnels. The big ones wore a similar uniform, but faded blue instead of grey; the small ones wore the same kind of loincloth. Mostly they were seated with their own kind, but there were a couple of groups in which both faces were sitting together. The big beasties were arguing, some of them shouting, making threatening gestures, baring their teeth. It looked like a fight might break out any minute.

The small beasties in loincloths weren't arguing, but they were just cringing in the corners, as though they were frightened and didn't know what to do. I had never seen the small beasties *not* working before.

The beasties had always been so regimented. Their confused and disorderly behavior now was strikingly different. This room was even dirtier than the tunnel outside. What had happened in the Coleville tunnels?

The new beasties kept turning to look at us, whispering to each other as they stared. Their expressions, with their round faces and big chins, were suspicious, hostile. And why shouldn't they be? They didn't know us. And they had good reason to be hostile toward humans today. One of them hissed as we passed. It had a transplanted human nose. Was it Mrs. Sloan's?

I was scared of them; I was sure Colette was, too, but we kept going, Colette clutching my arm, searching. I was really worried. Where was Fingers? What if something had happened to her in the battle? Why hadn't I thought of worrying about that until now? I guess I had imagined that she was safe because she was blind and would stay out of the fight. But now that we were down here, not finding her, I realized that, in the darkness of the tunnels, Fingers would insist on fighting, despite her eyes. If those loggers had done anything to her, I swore that I would get them for it.

"There she is! She's safe after all!" Colette said and pointed.

Fingers was sitting alone on the floor in a corner, slumped over. She looked even more haggard than usual. There was a bandage on her right arm. We hurried over, ignoring the Coleville beasties' nasty looks. "Fingers, it's us," Colette said.

Fingers lifted her head and smiled weakly. She cleared her throat. "I am happy you are able to coming back safely," she said, her voice gravelly.

Colette and I both started talking at once. "Are you okay? What happened to you? Were you hurt bad? Was it a bad fight? The ones we never saw before—are they from the Coleville tunnels?"

"They are from the tunnels near Coleville camp, where battle happen," she said, sounding tired. "Those tunnels now are abandon. We have to trying to make place here for those who once living over there. We are not knowing exactly how we will do it. But never anyone can staying in those tunnels anymore, ever ever again."

"What do you mean, no one can stay there? What happened?"

"Human males crashing down into the tunnels

there. First ones dying right away, under trapdoor. But more come. We hide, and waiting for them, and try to killing them fast and quiet." She hissed and ran her finger across her throat. "We cannot let any of them to leaving, to telling others about tunnels. But one man, he have small machine he can talking to someone outside, someone who wait and too coward to coming in."

Colette and I looked at each other. It had to be the boss who was waiting outside.

"So, yes, we killing those who come in—we have no choice. But we cannot go outside in the daylight and getting the one who wait there. We don't know how far away he is. Nothing we can do. And now, that *one man* knowing where is entrance to other tunnels," she said bitterly. "And so he will coming back, with more men and more brutality machines. And he will destroying those tunnels. Only thing we can do is making sure we are sealed off here. For safety first. But also because dead humans in those tunnels. Very very bad there."

"Are you sure you're safe here? They really can't get here from there?" I asked her.

"Yes. We taking care of that already—easy, because we never going over there for long, long time. But still very very bad thing, losing other tunnels.

Now not enough room here, not enough food. All more hungry than before." She lowered her voice. "And all because family over there showing tunnels to adult female human, who work at Coleville camp. Never trust adult human!" she said sharply. Then she sighed. "But they needing a human liaison to helping them at the camp."

"Mrs. Sloan," I murmured.

"Okay, you don't have those tunnels," Colette said. "But you can just dig more tunnels here to make room for the others, right?"

"Losing other tunnels—that not worst thing." Now Fingers sighed so deeply that her whole skinny body shuddered. "Queens die. Our Queen and their Queen, too."

Colette put her hand to her mouth. "No," she said. She shook her head. "You can't . . . but . . . how is that *possible*? How could the men find their way to the Queen's quarters, so far down, so hidden, so guarded? What went wrong?"

"Humans not go down there, not finding Queen. But both Queens old. Both Queens very fragility now, because so many trees gone, and fungus hard to find. Both Queens losing litter in last few days. Queens very much afraid. And very sickness for Queen to having so many human adult males in tunnels—and human death in tunnels. Housekeepers giving tea, but have to ration now. Not strong enough to stopping fearfulness of Queens. Not strong enough to stopping sickness of toxic human presence. Queens die." Her shoulders slumped. "Cannot imagine how to survival now. No one to lead, no one to follow in time of trouble, no one to stop the fighting. Queen live longer than anyone. Have our Queen for many many many generations. And now . . . gone."

All at once I had the answers to a lot of questions—answers so obvious I should have figured them out a long time ago.

The Queen was the only one who could have children—I had begun to realize that last night. Now I saw more clearly that they were like some insect colonies I had seen on a nature TV show. Everybody in the colony had a specific role to play, a job to do. The larger beasties were soldiers; the smaller ones were housekeepers. The Queen's job was to keep everything in order—and produce offspring.

Fingers said they'd had their Queen for many, many generations. So not only did everybody in the colony have the same mother; after several generations, the Queen would have only her own offspring to mate with. That was why they all had the same face. They were incredibly inbred.

The whole idea of it was gross, in a way. I knew from a show about ancient Egypt that inbreeding was very unhealthy in humans—it ended up producing idiots, monsters.

The beasties weren't human; a certain amount of inbreeding was obviously natural to them. But maybe they were inbreeding more than was good for them now, because they were more isolated, separated from other families, hiding. Fingers had said several times they never went over to the other tunnels anymore. Maybe what was wrong with their bodies wasn't *only* the forest being cut down, forcing them to ration their special tea. Maybe there was another reason, too. And that gave me an idea.

"So, will be fighting now," Fingers was saying. "If only one Queen, all would follow. Queen can give direction, telling all what to do in time of problem—everybody do what Queen says. But because no Queen, both family wanting new Queen from *own* family. Do not have one person strong enough to claim right to be Queen. Will never decide. Fighting among ourselves more terrible than fighting from humans."

"Fingers," I said. "Listen. What if . . . what if the two families mixed? A Queen from one family and her mate from the other one. Wouldn't that make it easier for both sides to agree? And wouldn't that make stronger babies—babies who wouldn't die? Babies who wouldn't lose their limbs?"

Colette was staring at me. Was it because I had said something brilliant—or something shockingly wrong?

And then Fingers nodded slowly. "Very good thinking, Doug. That why I let you live. Very good brain." She smiled a little. "I have same idea, too, so I *know* good idea. But nobody listening to me. Too afraid now to thinking."

"But what if *you* were Queen, Fingers?" Colette said. "They'd listen to you then. Everybody knows you're a good leader and smart and strong. You don't have the disease that destroys bodies. You're young. You know the tunnels better than anybody. The other family must have heard about you, too. Couldn't *you* be the one person strong enough to claim the right to be Queen?"

"Other family knowing about me, yes. Maybe even accept me for Queen, if I breeding with one of their males. Would be very good for all." She shrugged. "Only problem: Cannot be Queen with no eyes. Queen must pushing everybody around. Queen must have eyes."

"But the Queen is so much bigger," I said. "You say somebody can *become* the Queen? She's not born that way?"

"When old Queen die, everybody in colony is deciding who will be new Queen. After decide, new one go down deep inside earth to special territory of Queen. Living there, drinking strong tea. And changing, growing, happen automatic—can have babies now. But never pick Queen who can't see."

I thought of something. "Wait a minute. What about the people who died today? Humans *and* family who died. Couldn't you take eyes from them? And other parts, too, for people who need them. It doesn't make sense to waste their parts."

"I know you are trying to help, Doug. But don't understanding. Cannot taking parts from dead—can only do it if taking minutes after they die, and today, in battle, no time for that. In only few minutes, dead part no good anymore. Cannot using any who die today."

"Couldn't one of the family give you one of his eyes? Because you are strong enough to be Queen. For the good of everybody."

"Cannot taking any good part from one of us. Because so few whole ones left. Needing all we have."

"Well, then, what are you going to *do?*" I said, my voice rising. "You can't just give up! You can't just . . . go extinct. There's no one else like you! You have to get organized about food and shelter.

You have to keep fighting the logging companies. You can't just . . . just let yourselves stop going on."

"Many problems now," she said hopelessly. "Do not know what we will doing without Queen." Even Fingers was demoralized because there was no Queen.

The arguing voices were louder now. Some of the beasties were pawing at the earth in a threatening way, others backing away, hissing.

And then I had another idea. It would have been unthinkable even an hour before. But now, here in this situation, it seemed the obvious and only thing to do.

And Fingers had saved my life.

"Fingers," I said, feeling my heart thudding. "Do you think, if you could see, they would accept you as Queen? Really accept you?"

"But I cannot see, so why even asking me this?"

"Just answer me. Would they really accept you? The family from Coleville as well as your own family?"

"Well, I am second to Queen, even with no eyes. If could seeing, I think, yes, very logic I can be Queen."

"Then that's the answer," I said.

"What you mean? I don't understanding," Fingers said, puzzled.

But Colette understood now. She was staring at me with her mouth hanging open.

"You will be able to see, Fingers," I said. "Because I'm giving you an eye."

fifteen

"You . . . want to giving me an eye?" Fingers murmured, an unreadable expression on her face.

"Don't even try to argue. A lot of people only
have one eye, and they can see okay. And remember,
I have good eyes. I drew the map of the camp. I knew
all the right distances."

"Judging distance requires two eyes," Colette
pointed out, pushing her glasses up on her nose.

"Oh, be quiet, Colette," I said. But it did make

me think. With one eye, I might be able to see well enough. But probably not well enough to be good at baseball anymore.

"You . . . you really mean this, Doug?" Fingers asked me.

"Yes!" I said almost angrily. "You did something for me. Now . . . I can do something for you. You didn't ask me. It was my idea. I mean it."

Fingers reached out with her good arm. I took her hand. She squeezed, hard. "I did not making a mistake with you. You are miracle. And Colette, too."

And then, in an instant, she no longer seemed haggard. She got to her feet, swinging her head back and forth, listening. The beasties' voices were even louder, angrier. In the dim light you could see the spittle from all the hissing. Two large beasties stood facing each other, fangs bared.

"Hurry," Fingers said. "Not much time before very bad fighting. No time to wasting." She paused. "And if wait, I am afraid you changing your mind."

"I won't change my mind," I made myself say and gulped. Now that it was really about to happen—much sooner than I had expected!—I wasn't so sure anymore.

Colette and Fingers and I worked our way through the shouting beasties. They were all restless, moving around now. We had to guide Fingers. A couple of times we bumped into one, and it turned on us, hissing. Finally we made it out into the muddy tunnel and started up toward the operating room, Fingers in the lead.

"Well," Colette said. "You used to be so mean to me, Doug. And now you're going to lose an eye. You might call it poetic justice."

I didn't know what she meant by "poetic justice," and I didn't care. "What's the matter?" I said. "Are you jealous because I'm the one who's making the wonderful sacrifice? If you really wanted to help, you could give them one of your hands or a leg."

"I'm too small."

"Great excuse," I said.

"Children, do not arguing," Fingers said from ahead of us. "Too many things to worrying about now. Be nice."

We didn't talk for the rest of the way. I did my best not to think. About what it was going to feel like. How good the anesthetic was. How clean their equipment was. Not to mention Mom and Dad. How on earth were we going to explain *this* to them without giving anything away?

The beastie pumping away on the bicycle looked exhausted as we passed. They were cleaning up in the operating room, just having finished dealing with the wounded. There was a doctor and a nurse from each family; they seemed very tired. Fingers quickly explained the situation to them.

The doctors looked blank for a moment. Then they turned to each other, then back to Fingers. They spoke briefly, shaking their heads.

"Have not ever done an eye before," Fingers explained to me. "Are not knowing if it is possible. And are very, very tired. You are still . . . wanting to do this?"

For a moment I wanted to grab this chance to back out. What would be the point if the eye wouldn't work? But, looking at Fingers, I knew it was too late to back out now.

"Yes. I . . . uh, want to try it anyway," I said in a very small voice and nodded at the doctors.

The doctor from our tunnels went to a case and pulled out an old, fat book. It laid the book down on an operating table and thumbed through it until it found the right page—the page about eye anatomy. The book had to be way out of date. Both doctors bent over it. Both sighed deeply.

Fingers argued with them again.

The doctors shook their heads. They turned away and began washing their hands in brackish water in an old, rusty basin, using a lump of something black that I hoped was soap. The water sure didn't look clean.

One of the nurses moved the book and gestured for us to get up on the tables.

I looked at Colette. She wasn't smug anymore; she was scared. Then Fingers reached out and found my shoulder and squeezed it. "Whatever happen, Doug, I will never never forgetting this," she said.

Before I lay down, I saw the tray, with all sorts of sharp little knives and strange, frightening gadgets on it, including the hand-turned drill. Then the nurse was approaching with a syringe. I thought of how primitive the surgery was here, the beasties with lopsided noses and lots of scar tissue and one leg shorter than the other. Even if they got my eye out and into Fingers, what would be left of my face? How mutilated would I be? Was it too late to get out of this now?

The needle went into my arm. And soon after that, I was too sleepy to worry.

sixteen

I woke up feeling groggy. There was a bandage over my left eye and a dull pain back in there somewhere, but my right eye seemed fine. Colette fussed over me, asking me several times if I was okay, and I insisted I was. But as I got more awake, I noticed I had to keep turning my head to see things on the left; my field of vision was a lot smaller now. I could forget about baseball.

Fingers woke up soon after I did. Her head was wrapped in bandages.

But I won't talk about taking off her bandages. It's too clichéd. (Colette taught me that word.) So they took the bandages off, and Fingers could see with my eye. The doctors did a good job.

Fingers didn't seem groggy. She ran around the room beaming and exclaiming joyously, looking at everything. She looked for a long time at me and at Colette. She kept hugging and kissing us and the doctors and nurses, too. I was afraid she was going to knock something over. She could barely contain her excitement.

The doctors did seem pretty pleased with themselves, tired as they were. One of the doctors spoke to Fingers, making her look at her eyelid in a small, dull mirror. It seemed they hadn't been able to get the eyelid muscle to work. So they had attached a flap of skin and two snaps, one above the eye and one below it. The doctor showed Fingers how to snap it open and how to snap it closed.

"I love the snaps! I love everything!" Fingers cried out to us. And then she kissed me again. I could have done without that.

"How bad do I look?" I had a chance to whisper to Colette, while Fingers was hugging the doctors again.

"It's impossible to tell. The bandage they've got

on now is really big. No way to know what it's like underneath it."

"I just might have to wear a big eye patch, then," I said, thinking of Mrs. Sloan and her mask. I had turned myself into a freak. As happy as Fingers was, I couldn't deny that I was feeling pretty gloomy.

"What are we going to tell Mom and Dad?" I whispered to Colette.

"I'm thinking about it. We'll come up with something."

"Come. We go to showing the others. Stop the fighting," Fingers said eagerly. "Cannot *wait* for them to see me!"

We left the operating room. Fingers practically *flew* through the tunnels now. I felt very unsteady and had to go slowly. We got down to the big room many minutes after she did.

There were no angry voices now, only Fingers speaking as we approached the doorway. From the tunnel, we peered inside the room.

Fingers seemed to be outlining some kind of plan, counting things off on her fingers. My little blue eye looked odd in her face, with the flap of skin snapped above it. But nobody seemed to mind that. The eye worked. It was a miracle. The beasties were hanging on every word she said, in awe. That her sight had been restored seemed to be an omen—an omen that she should lead.

"She'll be a good Queen," Colette whispered to me as Fingers continued speaking. "She's so much younger than the last Queen. And she's kinder, too." Colette didn't have to explain how she knew that. The old Queen had wanted me killed; Fingers had decided otherwise. "And she's healthy," Colette went on. "She'll have good babies. She didn't lose her eyes because of their disease. She lost them . . ." Colette paused, thinking. "You know," she said slowly. "That gives me an idea."

But before I had a chance to ask Colette what she meant, Fingers looked over at the doorway and saw us. "Come here, come here, our dear friends," she said, beckoning. We had no choice but to step inside the room.

And then they were clapping, they were slapping the floor, they were hooting and crying out our names. Now they were really including me, not just Colette. And now I only had one eye.

It was a while before we got out of there. But as much as we dreaded dealing with Mom and Dad, we also wanted to get it over with. We went with Fingers to the upper level. It had to be the next day already. Mom and Dad would know we were missing.

"Be very careful now," Colette said. "They probably have people looking for us in the woods. You
mustn't let them find you."

"You think we don't knowing how to be careful?" she asked us jokingly. Nothing could upset her
now. "But I think best if you exiting through trapdoor. If parent are missing you, you cannot coming
up through basement of your house."

"I know. But what if there's somebody near the
trapdoor? What if they see us coming out?"

"I can check. We have spying place. And now I
can *see!*" she said rapturously.

It was in the room with the bicycle, the high,
narrow window between the ceiling and the wall.
Fingers climbed up the ladder and looked out.
Apparently from there she could see the trapdoor.
"Late afternoon. Nobody there," she said. "But go
quickly." And then, suddenly thinking of it, she
said, "But your parent? How are you to telling
them about eye?"

"I have a plan," Colette said. "Don't worry; we
won't give anything away."

"And I trust you will not," she said, meaning it
and grinning. And before we could climb up the ladder, she insisted on kissing us again.

Fingers followed us up the ladder, stopping before

she emerged fully. She had a little trouble squeezing her upper body through the trapdoor. Was she getting bigger already, because of the Queen decision?

The weather had cleared; the sky and the tops of the trees glowed in the warm evening light. Fingers looked around at it all with my eye.

"But . . . when you're Queen, you can never go outside," I said. "Once you get big, you'll be stuck down in the lower tunnels. Won't you feel trapped? Won't you miss . . . seeing this?"

She smiled. "With no eyes, can never going outside anyway," she said. "Better now." But as she started climbing down, she kept her eyes on the sky.

"Now, maybe to survival, because of you," was the last thing she said to us from the darkness inside. Colette carefully closed the trapdoor.

We walked, not speaking for a while.

Finally I said, "So what is this plan of yours about Mom and Dad?"

"First, we go all the way around, so we approach the house from the road, the opposite direction. Just in case anybody's watching from the house."

"Fine. But that's the easy part. What are we going to tell Mom and Dad?"

She meditatively rubbed her glasses. And I thought, If Colette didn't wear glasses, who would be missing an eye now? "We weren't out all night," she said. "We got up early to see the sunrise and to hike around. And then, a bird attacked you. A crazy bird. Just like what happened to Fingers. It just suddenly flew down out of nowhere and went for your eye."

It was pretty implausible, but I couldn't think of anything better. Certainly a crazy bird was more plausible than the truth. And it really *had* happened to Fingers. "What about the bandages? Who put them on my eye?"

"We were lucky. We ran into some backpackers. They had a first aid kit. They fixed you up and sent us right home."

I thought of something. "What about the boss? He didn't see any beasties, but he's got to know there was *something* down there killing his men. He'll tell people. What if they ask us about that?"

"We stick to our story. It was a bird. We know nothing about any tunnels or any weird creatures. Period."

We walked in silence. I had to keep turning my head to the left in order to see enough. Even so, I kept stumbling. It was going to take a long time to get used to this—if I ever *did* get used to it. What would Al think about my missing eye, I wondered vaguely. And it had all happened because . . .

I thought of something I'd been wondering about from the beginning. "Now that you trust me, will you answer a question?"

"What?"

"The book and the ball and bat," I said. "Way back when we first got here. I've been wondering about that. Where did they get them? How did they know we would like them? Were they really supposed to be gifts to lure us down there?"

"They took them from the house when the other people moved away. They thought they were children's things. So when they heard the activity around the house when we came, they put them out there, just in case some kids came along. Kids can help them better than adults; you know that."

"But how come they were two gifts that you and I especially like?"

She shrugged. "Beats me. Sometimes things work out that way, with the family."

But things did *not* work out with Mom and Dad. They were both hysterical about my eye. They didn't buy the bird story—even though Colette backed it up by reminding them of Mrs. Sloan and the ranger without an ear.

The state troopers were already looking for us.

"Tell them we're back; tell them to stop the

search," I said. "What can they do about a crazy bird, anyway?" I whimpered a little. "And after you tell them to stop the search, can't you please take me to the hospital right away?"

They couldn't argue about that. Dad drove very fast. I was a little worried that the doctors would wonder about the crude surgery on my eye. But it turned out they had seen other injuries like this— and weren't suspicious. "It's happened around here before," they told Mom and Dad. "Something goes wrong with the animals when the trees go." At least that helped to make our story a little more credible.

The doctors were able to clean up the wound a lot, in just a few hours, with local anesthetic. They even said that after several months I'd probably be able to be fitted with a glass eye, so no one would even know. In the meantime, they gave me a black patch. It made me feel like a pirate.

But even though the doctors said the accident was natural, nothing could convince Mom and Dad to let us stay here for even one day longer. It might have been different if Dad's research was going well, but he had been unable to find any *Aceropala* and had been about to give up anyway. They both wanted to get away from a place where accidents like this could happen, as soon as possible.

And they weren't dumb. They knew something else was going on that we hadn't told them. And they didn't like it. They watched us so closely while we packed that we never had a chance to sneak away and see Fingers before we left. We will probably never see her again.

What is going to happen to the beasties? Their situation is pretty hopeless. The humans have all the advantages. And when they can get the logging companies back in operation again, they will probably continue to destroy the forest.

And yet, somehow, I don't believe the humans will get *everything* they want. Not in Fingers' territory, anyway.